M

THE EAST AFRICAN MISSION

MARINE J: SBS

THE EAST AFRICAN MISSION

Peter Corrigan

First published in Great Britain 1997
22 Books, Invicta House, Sir Thomas Longley Road,
Rochester, Kent

Copyright © 1997 by 22 Books

The moral right of the author has been asserted

A CIP catalogue record for this book
is available from the British Library

ISBN 1 86238 004 X

10 9 8 7 6 5 4 3 2 1

Typeset by Hewer Text Composition Services, Edinburgh
Printed in England by Clays Ltd, St Ives plc

1

August 1978

It was a moonless night towards the end of the dry season, that three-month period of the year when the incessant rainfall around Lake Victoria lessened. The acacia and whistling thorn were in full leaf, the grass on the savannah as high as a man's waist. On the vast expanse of the lake itself colonies of birds bobbed, asleep on the waves. On the southern shore a few late lights glimmered in the town of Mwanza, in Tanzania, but most of the villages were dark and silent.

A series of dark shapes came hissing over the lake, long and sleek. They came from the north, from Uganda, the dictator-ruined country of Idi Amin.

The boats came on quietly and swiftly, their crews straining at the paddles. No outboards among them, they were powering towards the Tanzanian shore with only a whisper and splash of water, the starlit gleam of foam.

The old passenger steamer which served as their mother ship was five miles behind them. It had brought them from their barracks around Entebbe the night before. Lake Victoria has almost the same surface area as Scotland, and is subject to vicious storms. It would take a larger vessel than the open canoes these men piloted to cross her vast width – hence the old, hastily refitted steamer, a relic of colonial days, which waited now with her lights off and her engines turning over quietly, out on the dark expanse of water.

The canoes hit the beach, the men splashing out to haul them up the sand. A guard was left at each, hefting a Kalashnikov AK47 assault rifle. The rest of the crews dispersed inland through the insect-loud night. They were young men on the whole, from the Baganda tribe which had given their country its name. Tonight they would be visiting members of the Sukuma and Makonde tribes, who predominated in Tanzania.

They were dressed in ragged, filthy clothing that might once have been combat fatigues.

Many wore wellington boots; others were barefoot. But they all carried AKs, with spare magazines slung round their necks in canvas slings. Nearly all also bore a *panga*, the wicked machete of East Africa, and at least two had rifle grenades extending from the barrels of their Kalashnikovs.

They flowed inland like a silent pack of hyenas sniffing for blood.

All around the shores of the great lake were the scattered villages of fishermen, for the most part composed of round huts, thatched with brush and mud-walled, though some were reinforced with corrugated iron. Many of the villages were surrounded with thorn *bomas* to keep out the larger predators which roamed the wooded savannah beyond. The Ugandan soldiers poured into the villages with their *pangas* drawn and AKs cocked.

There were screams in the night, an isolated shot followed by a volley, a burst of automatic. Someone had grabbed a burning stick from a fire and was torching buildings. The night was soon lit up with crackling flames and the flash of gunfire.

Figures ran in and out of the darkness. Women shrieked as they were dragged from their beds to witness their husbands being shot or hacked to death. The Ugandans fired wildly at anything that moved. Screaming toddlers were cut in half by the heavy 7.62mm rounds. Old people were dragged out of their huts and chopped apart. The younger women were raped again and again by mobs of grinning soldiers, then shot where they lay.

The fires spread. The dried-out thorn of the *bomas* caught like tinder, forming circles of fire and trapping villagers within their confines. The raiders fired hundreds of rounds into the fleeing shadows trying to escape into the night, some hitting their own men. Then they began to retreat towards the lakeside, dragging with them the prettiest women and anything of value which caught their fancy.

They left behind them a series of raging infernos that lit up the shoreline for half a mile. Once back in their canoes they laughed and sang and plied their paddles with a will. The burning villages created a red glow in the sky behind them, and the dark shapes of bodies bobbed like corks on the calm waters of the lake.

The sun was already high in the sky, blazing down pitilessly on the shining water, when the canoes came to congregate once more around the patient steamer to the north. The men clambered up the rust-eaten sides of the old ship, tired now, their rifles hanging from their shoulders. They passed up the captives and the loot from their night raid and made the *sese* canoes fast to lines at the steamer's stern.

The boilers were stoked, steam raised, and the old ship began powering north again, to the Ugandan shores of Victoria. The white man on the bridge listened, grinning, to the account of the night's doings. His employers would be pleased, which was just as well. When the head men in Idi Amin's Uganda were not pleased, others' heads had a nasty habit of rolling.

He would refuel at Entebbe, which, ironically, had once been the main gathering point for the war canoes of the Ugandan kings, or *Kabakas*. Then no doubt he and his little army would be sent out to terrorize the Tanzanians once more.

It was all part of some larger scheme, of course. Amin was planning something big for which these raids were only a preparation. But the steamer's captain cared nothing for that. He was making a handsome profit out of the spoils of his nightly outings. People might be suffering, but then Africa had always been a harsh place, and no one would ever be able to change that.

2

The room was huge, wood-panelled and high-ceilinged. There was expensive carpet underfoot, a walnut drinks cabinet, Chippendale chairs, a vast desk. The telephones on the tooled-leather desktop seemed out of place, too modern for such a setting. Through the double-glazed windows, the faint hum of Whitehall traffic could be heard.

The man who sat behind the desk was Savile Row smart, grey-haired and double-chinned. Opposite him another sat in dark naval uniform, the cluster of rings on his lower sleeve marking him out as a rear admiral. His cap sat on his lap. He was frowning.

'I really can't see what it has to do with me, sir,' he said.

The man behind the desk steepled his fingers.

'I thought I had made myself perfectly clear, Admiral Leighton.'

'Oh, you have – perfectly. But I don't see what use I can be to you. Why not SAS? Or regular army? I cannot see the sense in getting the Navy involved in this. The situation seems volatile enough, and Marines would be working entirely outside their normal role.'

The man behind the desk sighed.

'Let me recap for you, Leighton.'

'It's Africa . . . I mean, why should we want to have our people in there in the first place?'

The other man's face darkened. 'If you will kindly let me explain.'

'By all means.' Leighton folded his arms and looked patient.

'We have reliable intelligence out of Uganda. Amin's regime is tottering. The madman has gone too far. It's all very well slaughtering thousands of innocents, but when a dictator neglects to pay his army, then he is courting disaster. Our information is that his army is mutinous and getting out of control. Amin has conducted a purge of many of his ministers and senior officers, and tried to buy off more through promotions, but he may have used that tactic once too often. There has been

8

more than one assassination attempt on him in the past six months, and it looks as though he may well be ousted by force in the near future . . .'

'Excellent news. The sooner that butcher is gone the better.'

'Quite, so long as another, worse butcher doesn't replace him. But I've not reached the important part. We have a source in Kampala, a reliable source, who seems quite adamant that Amin is planning a war.'

'Who with?'

'We're not sure. But all the signs point to an invasion of either Tanzania or Kenya. Now we know he has the hardware for it; Gaddafi has been supplying him with all things military for years now. The Ugandan Army is ill-disciplined and faction-ridden, but it is the best equipped in East Africa – all the latest Soviet equipment. Amin, it would seem, intends to unite it behind him by leading it on a victorious campaign either to the south or the east. No doubt the soldiers will extract their own wages out of whatever unfortunate country they occupy. And the Amin regime will have the resources of that country to draw upon.'

'God help us,' the admiral murmured. 'All East Africa under the heel of that madman.'

'Indeed.'

'I still can't see why you want Navy personnel for the job.'

'I'll explain. We have approached both Arap Moi of Kenya and Nyerere of Tanzania, to see how they would view the possibility of a small British training team helping their own forces – what there are of them.'

'And?'

'Moi refused. He's still trying to measure up to the memory of Kenyatta, and the last thing he wants is to start inviting the forces of the old colonial power back on to Kenyan soil. So there is nothing we can do there – though we have warned him of the current situation.'

'He'll be screaming for the UN if Amin's tanks begin rolling across his borders,' Leighton said grimly.

'Probably. But that is no longer our concern. The thing is, Nyerere, despite his Marxist leanings, has agreed to accept a small British presence. Apparently Amin's forces have been hitting his borders pretty hard this past few months, and Tanzania's army amounts to a few hundred barely trained militia. He's worried, quite rightly.'

'So we send in a team. But will that really make such a difference?'

'It depends who they are, Admiral. And this is why you are here with me this morning. You see, you may have forgotten, but most of the border between Uganda and Tanzania runs across Lake Victoria, and it is across the lake that the Ugandan forces have been making many of their raids. As well as training Tanzanian soldiers, Nyerere wants these raids curtailed and the invaders given a bloody nose. He thinks that if we can give Amin's thugs pause for thought down there, they may leave Tanzania alone.'

Leighton raised an eyebrow. 'And invade Kenya perhaps?'

The other man shrugged. 'That is not our problem at the moment. We can tackle only one bushfire at a time.'

'If I remember, it was you people who started this one, along with the Israelis. You couldn't get Obote out and Amin in fast enough.'

The suited man's eyes narrowed. 'We did what we thought was right for British interests at the time. We had no way of knowing that Amin was such an amoral psychopath.'

'How many of his own people has he killed now? Ninety thousand? And that's old intelligence. It could be a couple of hundred

11

thousand by now. And Britain helped put him in power.'

'I am sure I need not remind you, Admiral,' the man behind the desk said icily, 'that politics is hardly your arena of responsibility.'

'Oh, I know that. My kind, we only do the cleaning up after the politicians have finished their meddling.' The admiral glared at the other man. After a moment, however, he cleared his throat and said in a calmer tone, 'But I see now why you want a water-borne force. It would increase their mobility, for one thing.'

'What can you give me exactly? We need only two teams at most. Eight men.'

'I have 2SBS sitting in Poole. They'll be able to find the men.'

'Excellent.'

'What kind of political mandate do we have for this operation, though? Just how much support will these teams have?'

'Don't worry, Admiral. We have contacts in Tanzania in the Front for National Salvation. Tito Okello is their leader, and claims that he can put two thousand men at our disposal, all Ugandan exiles.'

'What about Obote? He's still in Tanzania. Won't he want to become president again if Amin actually falls?'

'Yes, but the Ugandan exiles in general have little to do with him. It was dissatisfaction with him that led to his fall from power in the first place.'

'Have they a viable alternative?'

'That is not a matter of import at the moment. The important thing is that these teams of yours will not be sent into a vacuum; they will have contacts and a ready supply of trainees.'

'And what about support from the UK?'

'We will back them up to the hilt, Admiral.'

'Will you, though? What about the Foreign Office? I take it they're on board.'

'This has been authorized at the highest level, I assure you, Admiral.'

'Bypassing the FO?'

The civilian's face reddened. His eyes glittered with anger. 'That is not your concern. This comes from Number Ten. That's all you have to know. One of my department heads will be round to brief your people as soon as you have selected them, and if you have any further queries then they are to be addressed directly to me.'

Leighton rose and settled his cap firmly on his head.

'MI6. You people just adore playing cloak-and-dagger, don't you? I'll go along with it – just so long as my men are not left with their arses hanging in the wind.'

Then he turned and left, ignoring the hand the other man had stretched out towards him.

3

Sergeant John Willan was tired, wet and cold. He was wearing a Surface Swimmer's waterproofed suit made of rubberized Grenfell fabric, and over it a waterlogged set of webbing that held his equipment. From one hand dangled a silenced Sterling sub-machine-gun and with the other he was pulling along a Klepper collapsible canoe, the rubber hull leaving a deep groove in the mud-flat he was squelching through.

It was the middle of the night on a desolate portion of the south coast of England and there was a bitterly cold wind blowing over the mud-flats and quicksands that stretched out behind him. The sea was a thin white line of surf a hundred yards back in the darkness.

It was two years since Willan had left Oman with the last of 42 Commando, but even now he still sometimes missed the hot sun of the desert, conveniently forgetting the bitter nights in the mountains. Especially now. It was supposed to be late summer, and yet he was having to stifle shivers as he hauled the Klepper up the muddy beach to the dunes beyond. Other grooves in the mud told him where to go; he had been the last man out of the submarine.

He found the rest of the section sheltering behind a slab-sided sand-dune, fanned out in All Round Protection. He dumped his own canoe and as he walked into the middle of the circular formation he yawned and said in a low voice: 'Endex then, lads. Any word of the transport?'

'Over the side of the dune, Sarge, engine running,' someone said to him in the same quiet tone.

'Any problems, boys?'

'Parker's boat leaked air a little; put him off balance.'

'What about debussing?'

'No problems, Sarge. We all rolled off her like shit off a shovel.'

'Good news. Grab your gear then, lads. Corporal Geary, do a quick kit check. We'll have a formal debriefing back at base. I want everyone out of the cold ASAP.'

'Fucking British summers,' someone muttered resentfully.

The section began gathering their equipment together. Willan collared the signaller and sent word to Zero, or Exercise Control, that he had called endex. It hadn't been much of an exercise really, more a revision of skills they needed to relearn every so often. They had been dropped by a P-class patrol submarine eight miles offshore and then paddled the Kleppers in through a rising swell. Old canoes, the Kleppers, in service for decades. They were kept rigid by being pumped up with air, and when deflated could be carried in a suitcase. It had been a while since Willan and several of his men had handled a paddle, so when the sub's commander had very kindly volunteered to carry the SBS section, it had seemed too good a chance to miss, despite the fact that it was at too short notice to book a training area. Willan was wondering now, though. The men seemed a little switched off, and if truth be told, so was he. He had almost finished his tour of duty with 2SBS; soon he would be going back to a Commando. He would miss the squadron more than he cared to admit. It would have been nice to wind everything up with a little live op, or a quick tour somewhere rather than this tame series of exercises they had been doing lately.

The red tail-lights of the four-tonners could be seen off in the dunes, their exhausts plumes of scarlet-tinted fog. It would be good also to get back to base, have a hot bath and then sink a few beers. Willan saw that all his men had gathered together and then led them off towards the waiting trucks. They were mostly silent; the eight-mile fight against the choppy sea had been exhilarating but tiring. They needed something to pick them up, he thought, a shot in the arm.

Or a new NCO maybe, he accused himself sardonically. He trudged towards the waiting transport in a black mood, thoroughly dissatisfied with himself. A good excuse to get rat-arsed.

Later the next evening, sitting in the bar with a frothing pint of bitter in his big fist, life seemed a little more rosy. Some idiot was playing 'Edison Lighthouse' on the jukebox, a couple of his section were having a game of pool and a few more marines were propped against the bar of the Globe and Anchor engaged in lively conversation.

Willan was something of a loner socially. He

had his friends, and he was a good team player when the occasion arose, but there were times when he seemed to put out invisible signals that said he wanted to sit in solitary thought. His section had long since gotten used to his minor eccentricities. They called him 'Dad' sometimes, only half in jest, for he was five years older than any of them, having got his SC3, his Swimmer-Canoeist qualification, in his early thirties. And now he was leaving the unit.

He drained his pint, held up the empty glass wordlessly to the attentive landlord, and lit a cigarette. He smoked rarely, knowing what effect the things had on fitness, but there were times when nothing else would do, and this was one of them.

The door to the pub opened and Mick Morgan walked in, a man so big that he made even Willan look diminutive. He spotted his sergeant and immediately made a beeline for him.

'Will! Scuttlebutt just heard.'

'What is it, Mick?'

The bigger man lowered his voice and leant close.

'The grapevine has it that there's an op on,

somewhere in sunny climes, and 2 Squadron is providing the bodies.'

Willan straightened. 'Where'd you hear this?'

'In the NAAFI. I brown-nosed the chief clerk. It's all black as hell, need-to-know and all that, which means, of course, that every fucker except us knows what's happening.'

'Any details?'

Morgan winked. 'Fancy going on safari, Will?'

'You're shitting me, Morgan.'

'No – straight up. Rumour Control has it they're wanting two four-man teams for a little sneaky-beaky stuff down where the lions roam, to help out our colonial brothers, as it were.'

'Fuck me pink.' The cigarette burnt forgotten in Willan's fingers. 'We're the only section actually in barracks at the moment. Three section is running about on Dartmoor, and One is doing that dive off the Lizard. Christ, Mick, it could be us.'

The big SBS man was grinning from ear to ear. The pool players had stopped their game and were watching Willan intently, smelling what was in the wind.

'I'll bet you a pound to a pinch of pigskin

that we get a Warning Order tonight,' Willan said, eyes shining. 'Mick, get hold of Willy Geary, and get together all the lads. I want them back in barracks early this evening, just in case.'

'They'll love that, Sarge.'

'Let them piss and moan. I'm not going to let One or Three get even a sniff of this little plum.'

Sure enough, the Warning Order came through that night. Seventeen years in the military had sharpened Willan's intuition as far as operations were concerned.

The section was placed on a three-day Readiness to Move, and Christmas arrived early, with great piles of equipment being issued to the eight men. Tropical combats were among the gear given out, confirming Rumour Control and Morgan's predictions.

As well as the High Power Browning 9mm handguns which were standard issue to all British Special Forces, they were also issued with the new Ingrams 9mm machine-pistol. Twenty-two centimetres long and weighing only 1.6kg, it can fire twenty rounds in a second. With the weapons came suppressors to eliminate flash and cut noise. Willan and his men spent a day on the range familiarizing themselves with the deadly new weapons, as happy as boys who have been let off school. They were warned, however, to keep consumption of ammunition to a minimum, and to fire on automatic only as a last resort. They would be given other weapons when they reached their destination, and the Ingrams were to be kept for special missions and last-ditch situations only. That little snippet of advice left the SBS men looking at one another. For the first time they wondered what they were really getting into.

They were to take Klepper canoes with them, but also four 'Rigid Raiders' with 35-hp outboards, each of which could have carried the entire section. Each man was also given a two-piece tropical diving suit and Mark II fins along with his standard diving equipment, and packed away in metal boxes were large quantities of 'Willy Peter', or white-phosphorus, grenades, and limpet mines.

'What are we going to do down there – fight a bloody war all by ourselves?' Willy Geary asked.

Some of their questions were answered at the final briefing. They had been jabbed full of vaccines by RAF doctors and informed endlessly about the wonderful diseases and local flora and fauna that awaited them. Then at last they found out that their destination was Tanzania.

They were to be flown in to Dar-es-Salaam by Hercules and from there transported to the town of Mwanza on the southern shore of Lake Victoria. There their mission would become twofold. They would set up a training camp, acting as though they were one of the old British Army Training Teams which had been so successful in Oman, and they would have a large number of Ugandan exiles and Tanzanian militia to lick into shape.

While this was going on they would also make their own analysis of the situation in the country and report back to London through a contact who would make himself known on their arrival. If circumstances warranted, and they probably would, they would then embark on operations across the lake to chastise the Ugandan raiders who were currently terrorizing the lakeside towns of Tanzania. Their discretion was relied upon, which made Willan snort with amusement.

It was a warm, late-summer afternoon and the briefing room was stiflingly hot, reminding the SBS men of what their destination would be

like. The man giving the briefing wore civilian
clothes – a shirt with sweat stains darkening
the armpits, and a tie. He had not introduced
himself except to say that he was authorized
to answer all their questions, and that nothing
inside the room would ever go outside it, until
the team was in Tanzania itself. The SBS men
were left feeling uneasy and irritated. The man
was obviously a 'spook' from Intelligence, and
he treated them as though they were a bunch
of untrustworthy children. Most of what they
needed to know they would find out when they
were on the ground, they were told. There were
good people there, already setting things up for
them. By the time they arrived in Mwanza the
camp would be well on the way to completion,
and supplies of armaments, ammunition and
equipment would be awaiting them.

'What kind of stuff do these Tanzanians
use?' Morgan asked, raising a hand.

'Soviet,' their briefer told him. 'AK47s,
AK74s, RPG7s, Dragunovs – you name it,
it's there.'

'No T-72s, though?' Willan asked with
a smile.

The civilian did not smile back. 'No. The
Ugandan forces have heavy Soviet hardware,
though it is badly cared for and the Ugandans

are inadequately trained. If the shit hits the fan, you can expect to come up against BRDMs, BMPs and old T-55s – we know that Gaddafi has supplied at least sixteen of those in the last year. We are also informed that Amin has at least sixty MiG 16s and 17s based at Entebbe which could be used for bombing all the northern Tanzanian ports. And France has also supplied him with eighty Savarin armoured cars.'

'Fucking Frogs,' one of the men muttered.

'What about the state of the Tanzanian military at the moment?' Willan asked.

'They have several hundred barely trained militia – basically a bunch of teenagers with rifles and little else. Nyerere has tried to give an impression of a population which will turn out and arm itself for any crisis, but it cuts no ice in Kampala. There are volunteers coming forward, however, and the Ugandan exiles are certainly keen enough.'

'No heavy weapons at all?'

'A few Second World War M3 half-tracks and a battery of ancient twelve-pounders. That's all.'

The SBS men shared dubious glances.

'And if the shit really does hit the fan, and

Amin invades, what do we do then?' Willan wanted to know.

'You will receive further orders once you are in-country to cover all contingencies. At the moment your mission extends only to the twofold responsibilities I have already outlined.'

'And we will receive these further orders from this mysterious contact of yours in Dar-es-Salaam.'

'Correct.'

'In other words,' Willy Geary said in a whisper, 'it's the spooks pulling the strings, not the Navy. Terrific.'

'Are there any further questions?' the civilian asked.

'Aye.' It was Jock Fraser, 'the marine from Aberdeen'.

'Yes?'

'Just how long do you expect us to be out there?'

The man in the sweat-stained shirt shrugged. 'Intelligence believes that if Amin does not invade by November, it'll be put off for another year. The rainy season will be in full swing by then, and the roads will be in such a condition as to bog down his vehicles.'

26

'A lot of Soviet hardware is amphibious,' Willan pointed out.

'True, but as I said before, the vehicles are not well maintained, and the troops will not like risking them. Amin needs a quick, clean victory. He will probably try to sweep down to the River Kagera and hold it through the rainy season, moving again once the rains have let up. He has to keep his troops on the move, and he has to give them easy victories. His main reason for the whole operation – if it happens, of course – is to head off discontent in the Army. It is his only power base in the country – without it, he's finished.'

'So if we bloody the nose of the Ugandan Army, Amin may fall?' Mick Morgan asked.

'Possibly.'

'What if we're captured?' Tim Breckenridge asked from the back.

His question seemed to startle the civilian.

'I cannot foresee that possibility.'

'But if it happens?'

'Then the British consul will make every effort to ensure your safe release.'

A wave of laughter swept through the room. 'With or without our knackers?' someone asked derisively.

Willan raised a hand to quell the mirth. It

was all too unreal – hard to take seriously. But that was a stupidly dangerous thing to do. A teenager with a Kalashnikov could kill as readily as a Spetsnaz. He resented the way his men were being drip-fed information, though. Clearly this was a 'black' operation. It would never appear in the papers, and if any of his men died in Africa he felt sure that their deaths would be put down to 'training accidents', as one or two SAS fatalities had been in Ireland. He had the uncomfortable feeling that he and his team were seen as expendable in the eyes of the man who was briefing them. There would be no back-up, unlike Oman, where RAF Strikemasters were on call, and where every effort was made to recover the bodies of dead comrades. The government would probably write off eight SBS men rather than suffer the indignity of trying to extract them from a bloody little war in Africa.

Still, it was what he and his comrades were paid for. They had volunteered for the SBS precisely because it gave them the chance to be involved in operations such as this. They had made their own bed; now they must lie in it. Thank God almost none of them were married – just Tony Parker out of the eight in the section. Perhaps that had even been a factor in the choice of his section – few dependants left behind, fewer awkward questions from grieving wives if the worst happened. It would not have surprised him.

'When do we leave?' he asked the sweating and obviously annoyed civilian who had briefed them.

The man cleared his throat. The room went silent.

'Tomorrow night. You'll fly by Herc from Brize Norton.'

Willan stood up. 'You heard the man, lads. I want everything squared away by noon tomorrow. Those of you who feel the need can wet your whistles with good English beer one last time, but God help you if any of you have more than two pints.

The briefing broke up. Unexpectedly, the civilian approached Willan and stuck out his hand.

'Good luck,' he said.

'I have a feeling we'll need it,' Willan retorted, smiling wryly.

The heat hit them like a wave. From the thundering of the Hercules they emerged on to crumbling tarmac in the dark of the night, with the lights of the airport off in the distance. They had landed at the runway farthest from the little terminal building. Willan smelt aeroplane fuel, dank air and a whiff of vegetation. Sweat began pouring down his back and sides as he walked down the ramp, Ingrams at the ready. There were trucks waiting for them there with their lights blazing, making him curse angrily. The roar of the Herc's engines drowned out his voice. Christ, it was hot, even at two in the morning.

Black faces all around him, grinning whitely in the headlights' glare. '*Jambo*,' they said cheerily, Swahili for 'hello'.

'Anybody speak fucking English?' he barked.

A man in old US Army fatigues came forward. He was lean as a wire, his face a smiling ebony mask. He held out a hand.

'John Kigoma. Very pleased to have you here, Captain. Come this way. My men will help you unload your gear.'

Willan followed him to the rear of the trucks. They were old American M35 Studebakers, looking as though they were held together by string and chewing-gum. He slung the Ingrams, waved at Geary as the SBS corporal glared suspiciously at the crowd of black soldiers, then bent over the bonnet of the nearest truck, where Kigoma had spread out a grubby map.

'See here, Captain. We load up all your things and we go down Pugu Road, turn left up Msimbazi Street and then we go out of the city, all the way. There is an old barracks about five miles out of town. There we rest up and pick up some men of mine. In the morning – or when it's light anyway – we set off for Dodoma, about three hundred miles. Three days maybe. Only at Dodoma are there railway cars which can take your boats and our vehicles. There we get on the railway, and you sit on a special train all the way to Mwanza, through Tabora – six hundred miles. Another three days maybe. It depends on the tracks. So you see, Captain, in one week we will be in Mwanza, maybe, and then we drive to the camp, which is just north of the town on the Mwanza Gulf, right on the lakeside.'

A week! The distances made Willan whistle softly. He had forgotten to take into account the fact that this was a primitive country, but also a vast one, where distances were measured in hundreds of miles. And he did not care for the number of 'maybes' in Kigoma's itinerary.

'We're supposed to be meeting someone here – a European. A civilian, I think.'

'Oh yes, Captain. That is Mr Prentiss. He is waiting for you at the barracks outside town.'

'Good. Let's get all the gear stowed away and get moving then. We don't want the Herc sitting here any longer than necessary.'

Most of the SBS section helped the local soldiers unload the big aeroplane, though Willan put Corporals Geary and Hill to patrolling the area around the plane as the process went on. The Rigid Raiders proved bulky but were heaved aboard the ageing trucks with brute force, as were the outboards. It took over an hour. The Hercules taxied away and one by one the trucks started up with coughing roars and great stinking clouds of exhaust smoke. Two SBS aboard each truck, weapons at the ready, and a crowd of Tanzanians hanging from every conceivable perch. The little convoy bumped off into the night.

Willan wiped the streaming sweat from his face. Welcome to Africa, he thought.

The outskirts of Dar-es-Salaam were quiet. There was not much night-life, Kigoma explained, except in a couple of big hotels that only tourists could afford. The whole place stank of badly kept sewers and the heat was like a soft blanket, even with the wind of the truck's passage. Willan could see clouds of dust billowing up in the headlights, and he could feel it settling on his skin, gritting between his teeth.

'Is it always as hot as this?' he asked Kigoma.

'No, not always. This is the dry season, from June to September. Rains will come in October for six months. You will wish it was back in the dry season again once October comes.' He laughed.

They left the city behind. The upholstery of Willan's seat was split and frayed and he could feel the iron frame underneath grinding into his spine. He winced as the truck lurched and shook its way over potholes. He slapped his neck as something bit it.

'Fuck. What about tsetse fly – much of it here down on the coast?'

'Oh no, thank the Lord. It is in the grasslands – the Serengeti, and up towards the Great Lake. Lots of sleeping sickness there a few years ago, but the people moved out. Nothing but lion and antelope and elephant there now.'

The trucks pulled up after what seemed an interminable time, the headlights illuminating a series of dilapidated buildings to one side of the road, and a sagging wire fence. Someone with a rifle came forward and Willan instinctively levelled the Ingrams.

'No no,' Kigoma said quickly. 'These are friends here. These are my men – the Tanzanian Army.' He called out something in Swahili and the man waved them on.

They finally stopped in a wide yard within the complex of buildings. As the engines stopped and the men jumped off the trucks Willan checked the luminous hands of his watch. Almost four. It would be dawn soon.

There was a quiet which seemed loud after the roar of the Hercules and then the trucks. He could hear insects by the million out in the bush beyond and, looking up, he saw a vast black arch of sky spattered with stars.

He shook his head, detailed Geary to set a watch over the trucks, then followed Kigoma into one of the buildings from which light was flickering.

A puttering Tilly lamp, a bare room with crude chairs and tables and a wrinkled poster of Julius Nyerere on one crumbling wall. Geckos clung to the cracked plaster, occasionally scuttling after insects. A man in a light-coloured jacket and trousers got up from the nearest table with a cigarette in his mouth and held out a hand.

'William Prentiss. Glad to meet you.'

Willan shook his hand. The man seemed deeply tanned, though it was difficult to tell in the light. He was thin as a reed and his hair fell down over his collar and ears. He might have been forty, but it was hard to say.

'Sergeant John Willan. My team are outside.'

'Good. Kigoma will show them somewhere to lay their heads for an hour or two. We start off just after dawn, and it's a long trip.'

'So I gather.'

'They measure distances in days here, as much as in miles, Sergeant. Kigoma is a good man. He's a colonel in the Tanzanian Militia, but he'll be acting as interpreter and general liaison officer for your men.'

Willan sat down, setting the Ingrams on the rickety table. Prentiss offered him a cigarette, but he declined. His mouth was too dry and the heat was too intense. Prentiss said something in Swahili to Kigoma, who was still hovering at the door, and the man left. There was talk outside. Willan heard Geary shouting orders.

'Who are you?' he asked Prentiss.

'I work for Six, as you've probably guessed. I've been out here since '70. I was in Kampala then – that was when Amin was the friend of both the British and the Israelis. He's firmly in the Arab camp now, and is trying to make Uganda into a Muslim country – what's left of it.'

'Is he really going to invade?'

'Oh yes. Tanzania, too. He and Nyerere hate each other personally, and Amin's regime will topple if he doesn't slip the army's leash. They stripped Uganda to the bone. Now they need somewhere else to play with.'

'What about this camp we were told about at Mwanza?'

'It's half-built. I'm told you'll have some two thousand men there by the end of the month, Ugandan exiles most of them, from about four or five different movements. There's the Uganda Action Group, the Uganda Group for Human Rights, the Front for the Liberation of Uganda, and the Front for National Salvation. Most of them hate each other only a little less than they hate Amin. And then there's Obote, of course, the ex-President. None of these movements want anything to do with him, but he'll not see himself left out of any wheeling and dealing.'

36

'Thank Christ I'm just a soldier,' Willan said with feeling.

Prentiss smiled. 'You and your men are supposed to be training these people – it'll be like juggling eggs.'

'I'll cross that bridge when I come to it,' Willan said, irritated. 'I was supposed to receive extra information from you concerning possible operations.'

'Indeed you were. And I have it – your first op.' He tossed a photograph on to the table. The SBS man squinted at it in the poor light.

'Looks like an old passenger steamer.'

'It's the *Victoria*, as you say, an old passenger steamer. But these days it's the mother ship for most of the Ugandan raiders who strike across Lake Victoria. They use the ship as a base and operate out of her in local canoes. The steamer is captained by a white man, Loos Van Dorn. He's an Afrikaner, a mercenary. Basically he and his little band of merry men have been playing merry hell with the Tanzanian shores of the lake.'

'How many?'

'He's supposed to have over a hundred gunmen in his pay, armed with light weapons – AKs and the like. Pirates, basically.'

'And we're supposed to take him and his steamer out?'

'Yes. Operation number one. Think about it while we're travelling to Mwanza. My superiors want him taken out as soon as possible.'

'And the training camp?'

'Oh, get it up and running by all means. But take out Van Dorn as soon as you can.'

Willan pocketed the photograph. 'Where does he operate out of?'

'Entebbe. The steamer lies up in the north-western islands of the lake while on . . . operations. We would prefer it if you did the business on her there as opposed to in Uganda itself. You don't want to give yourself too high a profile.'

'I see. And how are we supposed to locate her?'

'I fly Cessnas for a firm in Mwanza. We'll do an aerial reconnaissance as soon as my people in Entebbe send me word that she's put to sea.'

Willan considered it for a moment. He slapped a biting insect from his cheek.

'Seems straightforward. A little cowboyish maybe.'

'Get used to it – that's the way things are done

down here. Sometimes it seems as though half of Africa is run by seat-of-the-pants decisions. That, or the whims of madmen.'

'Charming. And what about Nyerere, the man who asked us here?'

'No one asked you here. You are not really here, and neither am I. That's rule number one. The President did not ask for Britain's help and does not know you exist – rule number two. He's not a bad sort, Nyerere, but he's full of ideals. The knowledge that he's had to ask for a helping hand from the old colonial master sticks in his craw – he'd rather that nothing happened to remind him of it.'

'So in other words my men and I are out on a limb in a big way.'

'Hell – it's what they pay you for, isn't it?'

Willan stood up. He was tired and irritable and suddenly aware that he disliked this man Prentiss and the entire set-up around him. But what he had said was true – it was what he was paid for.

'I have to check up on the men,' he said, and left the stifling room with the Ingrams dangling from one hand. There was a faint glow in the sky outside – dawn on his first morning in Africa.

4

Kigoma's estimate of six days had been decidedly optimistic. It took ten days to travel the nine hundred miles to Mwanza, and before the end of it Willan began to feel that he was not so much on a military operation as a nightmarish safari. The old trucks broke down continually on the non-existent roads and in places had to be unloaded and manhandled with brute force and the assistance of scores of enthralled villagers through quagmires, thick vegetation, rockfalls and rivers. When they finally boarded the train at Dodoma things improved a little, but the train had a habit of breaking down as well. Built by the Chinese only a few years before, the railway had quickly fallen into the disrepair and chaos that characterized the country as a whole. The natives took all the breakdowns and delays in their stride, sometimes making a party out of it at the side of the track, but for Willan and his men, chafing to arrive at their destination and get on with the job in hand, the delays were infuriating.

Finally they pulled into the station of Mwanza, almost on the shores of Lake Tanzania. There, more of the inevitable Studebakers were waiting and they unloaded and reloaded the equipment in what had become an almost automatic operation. Crowds of yelling children ran along the roadsides as the heavily laden trucks bumped slowly along and the Tanzanian soldiers travelling with the SBS men fired bursts of automatic fire into the air to add to the carnival mood.

'I don't fucking believe it,' Morgan told Willan. 'It's as if we're travelling to join a party.'

'Or a circus,' Willan added testily.

The camp, when they finally reached it, was situated just on the shore of Lake Victoria. The 'Great Lake' extended off limitlessly to the horizon, shining in the bright sunlight. There were fishing canoes out on the water, tiny as insects.

The camp itself consisted of a dozen buildings, constructed of brush and plastered with red mud. The roofs were of thatched reeds. They were built in a rough square, with a flat parade ground in their midst. From a warped flagpole the diagonal bar of Tanzania's national flag flapped idly. A goat was cropping the yellowed grass. The place seemed deserted.

'Home sweet fucking home,' Geary muttered, jumping down from his truck. Willan studied the place with a practised eye. It was a lot smaller than he had thought it would be – it would be hard to barrack two hundred men here, let alone two thousand. And the place was wholly without defences of any sort. Van Dorn's raiders might leap up out of the lake and burn it to the ground with hardly a struggle. Well, that would change.

Willan ordered Geary to unload the trucks and find a suitable hut for some of the gear. Then he asked Kigoma to show him around.

'Where are all the men?' he asked his erstwhile liaison officer. 'I thought they'd be here waiting for us.'

Kigoma grinned. 'No food here, no women – nothing to do. The men are in their villages. When you want them, they will come.'

'I'll bet,' Willan growled.

By that night he had the place organized after a fashion. He had established a headquarters office that doubled as a guardroom, an armoury, a stores building and sleeping quarters. He might be able to barrack a reinforced company here permanently, but the rest of his invisible army would have to sleep with the surrounding villagers.

He drew up a stag roster whereby one SBS man and a squad of six of Kigoma's men were patrolling the camp continually. There were rolls of rusted chicken wire in one of the huts, and with these he established a rough perimeter. Morgan and a couple of the other men rigged up a permanent vehicle checkpoint at the main 'gate' of the camp, and the locals built a little hut there for the sentries. Other villagers brought food for the new arrivals. The whole business was a logistical and administrative nightmare, but Willan threw himself into the work with relish. He told Kigoma to send out runners to the surrounding villages with orders for the would-be soldiers to parade at first light the next morning, bringing their weapons with them. Morgan was appointed quartermaster, much to the amusement of the rest of the team. Geary became adjutant. Breckenridge, a fitness nut even by SBS standards, was appointed PT instructor. Parker became the post's medical officer. The rest of the team would be training officers except for Jock Fraser, who was appointed chief scavenger. In Aberdeen Jock had had a tendency to appropriate items that were not necessarily his, before the Marines had sorted him out. Now that adolescent talent would be put to good use again.

Most of the team gathered round one of the cooking fires that night. Kigoma's men were roasting a haunch of something unmentionable and singing and laughing as they turned it over the flames on its spit. Willan stared into the fire, exhausted and deep in thought.

'Adjutant Geary – fuck me if this isn't Alice in Wonderland,' Geary said disbelievingly.

'I'll tell you what it is, Willy,' Morgan said authoritatively. 'It's an example of a civil servant tail wagging the military dog. What do you think then? Are we just the government's way of making a gesture? We haven't even got a proper officer with us, unless you count that Prentiss bloke. Now there's a spook if ever I saw one.'

Prentiss had left at Mwanza, promising to have supplies and extra equipment forwarded out to them. There was a rough airstrip to the south of the camp that had been hacked out

44

of the bush, but Willan did not know if the promised supplies would arrive by road or air. He knew bugger-all about anything, he told himself, and it annoyed him intensely. So far it had all been a bit of a lark, but at some point people were going to start getting killed and he was the one responsible for making sure that they were the right ones.

'Sending an officer with us would have given us too high a profile,' he said. 'I don't think we'll be getting any medals for this little op.'

'Well, we'll get a tan at least,' Keith Hill volunteered.

'What's the plan, Sarge?' Morgan asked. The SBS men went silent, listening.

'Well,' Willan said reluctantly, 'first things first. We get the camp up and running, see how many bodies we have to work with and what they're like. Then we start whipping them into shape. The Ugandan exiles are the most keen, apparently . . .' He looked sidelong at Kigoma, but the Tanzanian officer was nodding wisely.

'. . . and we'll see if we can't train up a few decent NCOs out of them. After that, we have a little job of our own to do.'

'Ah,' Geary said, satisfied.

'Then we await further orders from our

long-haired friend in Mwanza. He's our only contact in this country.'

'Will we be operating across the lake then?' John Gordon asked. 'I hope we haven't lugged those fucking boats halfway across the world for nothing.'

'Maybe,' Willan said cautiously. There were too many people around for him to say more.

The rough cots in the huts of the camp seemed like feather beds after days of sleeping in the backs of the trucks or in spine-jarring trains. Kigoma shook Willan awake at dawn and the sergeant dressed quickly, scratching the mosquito bites that covered his body and cursing his tiredness. The camp was already awake, and he could hear people talking outside, the shuffle of feet, someone shouting in Swahili. He buckled on his webbing and pulled his bush hat down over his head, then stepped out into the rising sunlight, checking the Ingrams as he did so.

Perhaps four hundred men stood there on the parade ground in uneven rows. They were mostly barefoot, dusty, carrying Kalashnikovs, old hunting rifles or shotguns. Many were armed only with *pangas*. They stood eyeing

46

the SBS men as Willan's team assembled before them. Kigoma and another man came up to Willan and saluted smartly.

'May I present Colonel Tito Okello, commander-in-chief of the Ugandan National Movement.'

'John Willan, Royal Marines,' Willan said, holding out a hand. He thought it better not to mention his rank, considering there were so many officers around.

'I take it these are the beginning of our little army,' he said, gesturing to the crowd of men shuffling on the dusty parade ground.

'They are my countrymen,' Okello said. He was a tall man, younger than Kigoma, and his 1960s-issue US combat fatigues were clean and well kept. A .45 automatic was holstered at his waist and he had an AK slung from one shoulder. He seemed fit, alert and intelligent.

'All the men you see before you were forced to flee their homes because of the excesses of Amin. Most have lost members of their families to his death squads. They will fight well, if they are properly trained.'

'That's why I'm here,' Willan said.

'But they need equipment, weapons, boots. Can you get them?'

'Yes,' Willan said, more confidently than he felt.

'Good! Then, Colonel Willan, they are entirely at your disposal, as am I.'

Willan turned to Kigoma, ignoring the other man's unwitting inflation of his rank.

'What about your people? What about the Tanzanian Army? I thought I was to have two thousand men to train.'

Kigoma shrugged, smiling ruefully. 'They are late, but they will come. They will be here soon.'

'Right,' Willan said. He wanted breakfast and a shower, but knew he was going to have to do without both.

'Let's get started then. Corp . . . Adjutant Geary . . . take the men's names and assign them barracks. Hill, Gordon, divide them up into training platoons. Morgan, I want you to get me a list of their weapons. Let's see what we've got to work with. And Parker, give them the once-over, medically speaking. Put down as fatigue men any who aren't up to scratch. Let's get to it, people.'

The SBS team immediately split up and strode off to their duties.

'Now, if you two gentlemen would join me in headquarters, I think we might benefit from

48

a little chat,' Willan said. 'And, Kigoma, if you could get someone to rustle up some breakfast for the men I'd be much obliged.'

Willan turned to watch just before ducking into the HQ hut. The parade ground was a hive of activity. Four hundred men – it was a better start than he had hoped for. All he needed now were decent weapons, uniforms, boots, supplies, ammunition . . . He shook his head. They'd muddle through somehow.

5

They came three nights later. It was a bright, starlit evening, and Willan's sentries saw the dark shapes of the canoes hissing towards them over the surface of the lake. Some idiot fired a volley of shots when they were still hundreds of yards away. A fusillade of automatic fire answered him, churning up the sand at his feet.

Willan ran out of his hut with the Ingrams levelled to find the camp alive with running figures. He bumped into Geary.

'What the fuck's going on?'

'Firing down on the lake shore. Looks like our friends may have decided to pay us a midnight visit.'

'Get the lads together. And for fuck's sake get hold of Okello. We've got to get the men organized or they'll end up shooting the shit out of each other.'

'Righto, Sarge,' Geary said, then dashed off.

Willan kept running down to the lakeside, cocking the Ingrams as he went. There were knots of the trainees down there, milling about. More shots. He saw the muzzle flashes out on the lake, answering fire from the shore.

'Hold your fire!' he shouted, hoping they would remember their brief training.

'Hold your fire!'

The firing sputtered out. Kigoma grabbed him out of the darkness.

'Captain, it is the Ugandan raiders. They have come!'

'I know. Get the men back off the beach, Kigoma. Get them into cover. Do you hear me? And no one fires until I say so.'

'Yes, Captain.'

The trainees were told to take up firing positions off the beach. Half of Willan's team stayed with them to make sure they stayed in position. The fire from the canoes continued. The Ugandans had hesitated on receiving gunfire from the shore and now were sitting in their boats and firing desultorily towards the muzzle flashes they had seen, as if they could not decide whether to abandon their mission and flee or press home the raid.

A moment later, however, they made up their minds. The firing stopped. They took up their paddles and began to head back the way they had come.

But by that time the roar of powerful outboards was filling up the night. Two Rigid Raiders manned by four of the SBS were powering out to sea in explosions of foam, their bows lifted out of the water by their speed. In one were Willan and Breckenridge, in the other, Fraser and Morgan. They closed in on the swarm of canoes like sharks moving in for the kill.

Wild automatic fire greeted them as the canoeists realized they were being pursued. The Raiders zigzagged in the water, their backwash making a confusing maelstrom of waves and surf which broke the rhythm of the paddlers. The Ingrams of the SBS crews spat out, almost noiseless compared to the noisy barking of the Kalashnikovs.

The Rigid Raiders carved great circles around the huddled mass of canoes, the SBS firing into the midst of the Ugandans, lobbing grenades into the crowd. Explosions sent fragments of wood and bodies flying into the air.

The return fire grew heavy. Several of the

raiders were shot by their own comrades as the occupants of the canoes fired wildly at the speeding boats. Willan could sense the heavy fire hissing over his head. His boat thumped as rounds struck it, ripping the surface skin. In the canoes, some bright spark fired an RPG, the back-blast roasting three men behind him, the missile creating a great fountain of foam as it exploded.

More bullets hit Willan's boat; in a few minutes he found he was low on ammo, having fired four full magazines into the paddling Ugandans. He thumbed the pressel switch on the PRC349 radio.

'Zero to One-Zero, break off contact. I repeat, break off contact.'

A moment later, Fraser's Scots burr replied reluctantly: 'Roger, Zero, breaking off now.'

The two boats zoomed away from the packed mass of canoes. Willan winced as the bow of the Rigid Raider bumped against bodies floating on the surface of the lake. The entire skirmish had lasted about six minutes from start to finish.

They beached the boats back at camp to find the trainees cheering jubilantly and jumping up and down on the sand, despite the efforts of the other four SBS men to calm them down. Geary marched over to Willan, furious.

'The stupid buggers think we've just won World War Three. You all right, Sarge? It sounded pretty hot out there for a while.' He fingered a bullet hole in Willan's vessel.

Willan was suffering his usual feeling of let-down after a contact. The adrenalin was leaking out of him, leaving him exhausted and muddle-headed.

'We couldn't press on – we hadn't the ammo for it, and it was too big a risk. It's too early yet to be charging in like the Seventh Cavalry. It was a mistake, Willy.'

'How's that?'

'They know now that something's up. They'll be prepared for us next time.'

Fraser splashed through the shallows from his boat, still wild-eyed from the fight.

'We could have taken the whole lot of them out, Sarge, or followed them back to that mother ship of theirs.'

'Bollocks,' Willan grunted. 'We gave them a bloody nose – that's enough for now. I'll bet we took out at least twenty of the bastards. But the mother ship will have to wait. No point in going off at half cock.' He turned to Okello, who was hovering nearby, listening in.

'For Chrissake, Okello, can't you get your men to shut up? They'll wake up the whole coast.'

Okello stumped off grumpily. They heard him shout harsh words in Swahili to the cheering trainees who were lining the beach. Gradually they calmed down and began filing back up to the buildings of the camp.

Willan patted his Ingrams, looking round at the other SBS who had gathered about him.

'From now on, we treat the ammo for these babies like gold dust. We were blowing it off out there like there was no tomorrow, and God knows if or when we'll be resupplied. I want you all to get hold of AKs, even if you have to take one off a trainee. The Ingrams are to be saved for special ops only. Is that clear?'

'Aye aye, sir,' Fraser said, grinning.

'You fucking Jocks – you just love a good dust-up, don't you?'

'It's mother's milk to us, Sarge . . . I mean, *Colonel* Willan, sir.'

Willan laughed. 'All right, back to camp. Let's get everyone settled down. We've a busy day ahead of us tomorrow.'

*   *   *

News of the lakeside battle spread quickly. In the morning there were another three hundred men standing on the dusty parade ground, eager to be part of the fun. Willan had enough personnel now to make up a good battalion, but he continued to organize the camp along company lines. The brightest and best of the recruits were taken away and put through a special training cadre designed to turn them into some form of NCO. Lacking uniforms, Willan gave these men white armbands as badges of rank and as far as he was able, made sure that they had the best of boots, weapons and clothing. They were to be the backbone of his little army.

A week went by. The supply problem continued to be a nightmare. There was no real logistical back-up for the men of the camp, and Willan was forced to use a substantial number of his trainees as scavengers, builders, cooks, labourers and so on. But the recruits continued to trickle in, and the camp grew in size. On the other hand, the weapons and rations that Prentiss had pledged him never arrived and a large proportion of the recruits continued to train with *pangas* and shotguns, dressed in rags. More than once, they all went to bed hungry. Willan fumed, sending off the old

Studebakers in rattling convoys to Mwanza for supplies and news, but little of either was forthcoming. The Ugandan raiders did not come back to the vicinity of the camp, but they struck at other stretches of the coast, their activities seemingly deflected but still unchecked.

Okello and Kigoma, Willan found to be good officers. The Ugandan exiles were keen as mustard to hit back at their renegade countrymen, and formed the core of Willan's rapidly growing NCO cadre. Soon they were ordering about the other recruits in their turn, and a proper military organization began to make itself seen throughout the camp.

Under Mick Morgan, the trainees built for themselves a system of foxholes about the complex, protected by rusting barbed wire. An assault course was constructed that formed part of every day's activity. The curriculum of daily events followed the tenets of basic British military training, with a run or session of callisthenics just after reveille, then a meagre breakfast, then a morning's training in weapons handling. In the afternoon small-unit tactics were taught.

While these disciplines formed the timetable for most of the trainees, the NCOs were taken away and taught on their own, with more emphasis on tactics and administration in the field. Finally, a group of the recruits were detailed every day for fatigue details such as guard duty, construction and 'foraging'.

The last became a real problem. Willan felt sometimes that the entire world had forgotten about the existence of the Mwanza camp. His foraging parties had to roam farther and farther afield in search of supplies, and after complaints of extortion and looting came back to him he had to send one of the SBS with each party to make sure that the trainees did not use their weapons to take what they wanted. But it was difficult. Despite the keenness of the novice soldiers to learn, they were irritated and annoyed – as was he – that they seemed to exist in a vacuum and received no support from the British government or the Tanzanian military to keep going. Kigoma himself was dispatched to Mwanza on more than one occasion to plead for arms and rations, but each time came back with empty promises that were never fulfilled. As for their 'contact' in the country, Willan swore that the next time Prentiss popped into view he would strangle the spook with his bare hands.

*　　*　　*

Eleven days after the skirmish with the Ugandan raiders, Okello came into headquarters to say that an aircraft was circling the camp. Willan went out into the blinding sunlight and looked up to see a small white civilian plane with a single-prop engine buzzing the roofs of the huts. He smiled grimly and called for a truck and a small escort.

They bumped through the bush to the little overgrown airstrip at the south of the camp, and there waited as the plane landed, lurching and jolting over the uneven surface. The propeller feathered to a halt and William Prentiss got out of the cockpit in a grubby linen suit, looking like something out of a Graham Greene novel. He waved to Willan, but the SBS sergeant stood with his arms folded, bush hat shading his eyes.

'I'm impressed, *Colonel* Willan,' Prentiss said, smiling. 'Sandhurst in the jungle, no less. You've made progress.'

'We do our best,' Willan said quietly. He and Okello stood unsmiling, not offering to help the Englishman with the two heavy bags he carried.

'I say, give me a hand, will you? These things weigh a ton.'

Willan waved a hand and two of the recruits

who had come with them picked up the bags and threw them into the back of the truck. They crashed down on the truck bed as heavily as if they were full of pig-iron.

'Now,' Prentiss said, quite unabashed. 'We have a lot to talk about.'

'You're right there,' Willan said drily as they boarded the truck together.

A little later Willan, Okello, Kigoma and Prentiss were sitting on the rough chairs in the HQ hut, drinking mud-coloured tea and listening to the regular crump of feet out on the parade ground. Prentiss's long, strangely heavy bags lay to one side. The MI6 agent seemed unperturbed by his frosty reception.

'Where have you been?' Willan asked, unable to rein in his impatience any longer.

'Oh, all over the place. Business is good – booming, in fact. I'm thinking of branching into tourism. Airborne safaris and the like . . . What bloody awful tea.'

'You get used to it,' Willan growled. Okello and Kigoma sat impassively. They could hear Fraser's Aberdeen accent shouting orders outside.

'I'll bet you do. Now, I'm sure you're all wondering why I'm so late . . .'

'And why we've received nothing in the way of supplies or equipment,' Willan interrupted harshly.

'Quite. Well, you have to remember that this is Africa, Willan. Everything takes time, and nothing is as simple as it seems. The Tanzanian government is a little leery of arming Colonel Okello's good men; it finds it hard enough to look after its own.'

'What?'

'Yes. By the way, congratulations on your little skirmish on the lake. The President found it most gratifying, I am told, though he seems to believe that it was native Tanzanian forces who took part in it.'

'And he's becoming less than willing to finance a project to arm and train forces other than those of Tanzania,' Okello added.

Prentiss shrugged. 'He seems to believe that Amin's projected invasion may not happen after all. He's quite willing to train a defensive force to protect the southern shores of Victoria, but I'm afraid, Okello, the prevailing feeling in Dar-es-Salaam seems to be that your men must look out for themselves.'

Okello scowled.

'That's just fine and dandy,' Willan rasped. 'But I have damn near eight hundred men to feed here, and many of them are Tanzanian. What do you want me to do, feed them and let the Ugandans go hungry? It's a recipe for mutiny. And how the hell am I supposed to train an army if half the men have no weapons or ammunition? Most of them are barefoot, for Chrissake!'

Prentiss held up a hand.

'No need to panic just yet, my friend. I come bearing a useful piece of information from the Tanzanian Army chief himself – unofficially, of course.'

'Well?'

'These raiders whose style you cramped in that abortive raid two weeks or so ago, they've been striking elsewhere now, avoiding this place like the plague. And they've been reinforced. Everyone is a little pissed off with it in Dar-es-Salaam. The unofficial feeling is that if you can wipe them out for once and all and capture – as opposed to destroy – their mother ship, then you'll have earned yourselves a little slap on the back, in the manner of weapons and ammunition and the like. Plus, of course, whatever you happen to capture on the steamer.'

Willan glared at the other white man angrily.

'*Capture* it? Do you have any idea what you're asking?'

Again, Prentiss held up a hand in a gesture that somehow conveyed a wealth of world-weariness.

'I am only relaying what is on the grapevine in official circles. I realize that to destroy it would be a lot easier, but I think . . .' – here he lowered his voice slightly – '. . . I think that the government would like your Ugandans, Okello, to take the war to their countrymen.'

'Do unto them what they have been doing unto us,' Okello said drily.

'Precisely.'

'Getting the Ugandan exiles out of the way and also hitting back at Amin. Two birds with one stone. How very convenient,' Willan said savagely.

'Don't shoot the messenger,' Prentiss said, a tinge of real irritation in his voice now. 'I'm as much of an errand boy as any of you.

'But that's it, is it? Either we capture the steamer and wipe out the raiders or we can wait until doomsday for any kind of equipment or support from the government.'

Prentiss shrugged.

'Terrific.' Willan bowed his head in thought.

'My men are at your disposal, Colonel,' Okello said quickly.

'And mine,' Kigoma added, breaking his long silence.

'And for what it's worth, so am I and my little air-taxi,' Prentiss said, grinning now.

'Do you know where the steamer might be at the moment?' Willan asked the MI6 agent.

'Roughly. It was last seen off Bukoba, to the north-west. Over a hundred and thirty miles away.'

'How much fuel is there in that plane of yours?'

'Enough.'

'Good. We'll take a ride out first thing in the morning and see if we can spot the bugger.'

'It's a hell of a big lake, Willan.'

'I know, but we've got to start somewhere. Once we've found it, we can start planning.'

'Fair enough.' Prentiss hesitated. 'There's one more thing I ought to tell you.'

'More good news?'

'That depends. How do you feel about the press?'

'What?'

'Word of your little operation here has got out. There are quite a few foreign journalists hovering about Mwanza trying to find out where the camp is. There are rumours of white mercenaries all over the town.'

'Great,' Willan said. 'Just great. This operation is going pear-shaped at a rate of fucking knots.'

'Just thought you should know.'

'I'll make up orders for disposing of journalists before we leave tomorrow. Christ, this is getting more unreal by the day.'

'This is Africa,' Prentiss said wearily. 'It's par for the course.'

Dawn came with the silent blaze of a vast rising sun, flooding the camp with orange light. Willan and Prentiss trudged out to the aircraft just as reveille was being sounded in the camp with its usual clatter of sticks on corrugated iron.

'What a bloody awful way to wake up,' Prentiss observed as half-asleep men tumbled out on to the parade ground by the hundred and the new NCOs bawled orders at the top of their lungs. The morning quiet was shattered.

It was more peaceful out by the crude airstrip. Once there, Prentiss popped open the aircraft's door and lugged a large plastic tank out of the cabin. Then he began refuelling the plane, for all the world like a motorist topping up his car. Willan looked the little aircraft over suspiciously. He was a marine, not a para, and distrusted aeroplanes on principle.

'How far will this thing take us?'

Prentiss lowered the fuel container, puffing slightly.

'Once we get there, we'll have about forty minutes over the area before we have to head back. I can refuel at the airstrip outside Mwanza, and then head north for another shot at it. It may take a while – like I said, it's an awfully big lake.'

'It might help to have someone on the ground as well, pumping the locals for information.'

'Oh, don't worry about that – it's not a problem. I have sources all over western Tanzania. It's where Amin will have to invade, you see – if he does invade.'

'If he does invade,' Willan repeated wearily. 'I sometimes wonder if all this is a joke cooked up by some mad pen-pusher in Whitehall.'

Prentiss shook his head. 'It's no joke, my friend. If Amin conquers this country he'll make it a hell on earth for these people. We can't let that happen.'

'You like it here, don't you?'

The MI6 man lowered the empty fuel container and wiped his brow; it was already hot, and flies were buzzing about his eyes.

'Yes, I do. This is one of the most beautiful countries in the world, and the people are as open and friendly as any I've ever met. It could be a paradise, if it was managed properly.'

'What, by the old colonial rulers, you mean?'

'No. They fucked up in Africa too. Look at the Congo. There's half a dozen wars just waiting to start on this benighted continent, most of them legacies of colonial incompetence. Tribalism is what is the ruin of Africa. It's always been here, but now they slug it out with AK47s and T-55s instead of with assegais and knobkerries. What the colonial powers did was to heighten the potential for genocide across Africa. Look at Uganda now; it's like an African Cambodia. And it was the British and Israelis who helped Amin into power.'

'And the Libyans who are keeping him there.'

'Yes. There's always some fucker who wants to keep the pot boiling.' Prentiss tossed away the empty tank.

'All done. Let's get going, shall we? Best

to take advantage of the early light. It'll get hazier as the day wears on.'

Prentiss's pre-flight checks looked decidedly perfunctory to Willan, and he belted himself into the tiny seat tightly. He had a Browning pistol at his hip which made life a little uncomfortable, and a pair of binoculars slung from his neck. When the engine started up he seemed to feel the vibration shaking up and down his spine. He wondered what it would be like to ditch this thing in Lake Victoria and play tag with the crocodiles, then put the image out of his mind. Best not to dwell on it.

The little aeroplane jogged and bounced along the crude runway and with a sudden, sickening lurch, was airborne. The T-wing configuration made for good observation, but also gave the impression that the passenger was on the edge of a vast cliff, with the ground speeding past at its foot. But it was exhilarating too. Willan relaxed somewhat, and tried to ignore Prentiss's persistent tapping of the artificial horizon gauge. It seemed to be stuck at an impossible angle.

There were no spare earphones for the passenger, it seemed, and so Willan had to endure the ear-aching roar of the engine and any conversation with the pilot had to be conducted at a shout. He resigned himself to it and the rumbling of his stomach. They had breakfasted on nothing but cold tea, gulped down in the half-light before dawn.

Sunrise had occurred with the speed customary in that country. The sun was well over the horizon now, pouring down on Willan's right side whenever the aircraft banked to port. He could see the first dots of fishing boats on the lake and the pink swarms of flamingos in the shallows. Peering through the binoculars, he studied the maze of small islands that studded the western shores of the lake. A veritable labyrinth of convoluted waterways, shining like silver in the sunlight. For the first time, he wondered if it might be possible to find one medium-sized vessel in the midst of all that, and shouted as much to Prentiss.

The Intelligence man nodded, slipping off one earphone.

'No good just to circle about and hope for the best,' he yelled in Willan's ear. 'But my information is pretty recent. Bukoba, that's what they said. It narrows the odds down quite a bit. And the steamer will be standing out to sea, remember. They won't risk it in among the islands.'

Yes. Willan had forgotten that. He scanned the lake with his binos continually, watching for the flash of white that would be the *Victoria*'s hull.

Thirty minutes after take-off, Prentiss nudged him and pointed down to the coast below.

'Bukoba!'

It was one of many such small, straggling lakeside towns, the lake front crowded with canoes and, behind it, what looked like a hiving market-place. Old pick-up trucks clogged the streets, along with cattle and crowds of brightly clad people. They circled the place once at five hundred feet, and Willan could make out the upturned faces, the pointing fingers.

'Look north,' Prentiss told him. He did so, training the binoculars to regard a massive expanse of bush and secondary forest, cleared fields, the red-brown of naked earth crossed by a single road. There was another town out on the undulating spread of the plain, smaller than Bukoba. Willan looked at his map. Kyaka. Just to the north of the settlement he could see the meandering curve of the Kagera, sluggish and brown. It looked more like a wide, shallow ditch than a river.

'That's Uganda,' Prentiss said, pointing at the land beyond.

'Christ, it's close, isn't it?'

'Less than thirty miles. You're looking at the Ugandan invasion route, Willan. Amin's tanks, if they come, will come down that road.'

They banked right and the aircraft curved in a graceful arc into the eye of the sun. She shuddered a little as she passed through some light turbulence, and then they were speeding out across the vast, glittering face of Lake Victoria. Willan kept the binos to his eyes as though they were some kind of extension of his face. He ignored Prentiss's tapping of the fuel gauge.

The little plane climbed to a thousand feet. The air was as clear as glass and Willan could see for miles. Prentiss, he noticed, was quartering the lake systematically with wide, right-angled turns.

They flew on in silence for twenty minutes until Prentiss tapped the SBS sergeant on the shoulder.

'We've just crossed into Uganda,' he told him.

Willan looked down again. There was no difference to the lake below; the boundaries so important on maps did not exist out here. But he remembered his briefing back in England, and frowned.

'Will they mind us entering their airspace?'

Prentiss grinned. 'They probably don't even know where their airspace is. Don't worry, Willan. They have no land-based radar capability down here, only around Kampala. And their MiGs don't make a habit of buzzing the lake. Not yet, anyway.'

They flew on. Time was running out, along with their fuel, and Willan's eyes were watering with the constant strain. He cursed under his breath.

There. A flash of white, like the back of a seagull, but farther away.

'Turn right,' he barked, and the little plane banked obediently.

Down there, somewhere. His eye had just registered it. He swept the area with the binoculars.

'Gotcha.'

The steamer seemed to be at anchor. There was a long, dark tail of towed canoes behind it, a wisp of smoke from the funnel. Probably they were keeping the fires banked.

'What's our position?'

Prentiss busied himself with compass and map.

'Got it. We're eight miles nor-nor-west of Bukoba. Bearing zero-six-three. Got the bastard.'

'Take us back. We don't want to arouse their suspicions.'

The aircraft turned sharply to the left and began a long curve that would put them back on the course to home.

'But how long will he stay there?' Willan asked.

'His SOP is to raid a shoreline for two or three nights running, with the mother ship standing off more or less in the same position. You can bet the bastards will still be there tonight.'

'And the raiders will be off in their canoes?'

'Almost certainly. Any ideas?'

Willan didn't answer. The beginning of a plan was forming in his head.

'We'll hit him tonight,' he said at last.

6

'Slow engines to one-third,' said Loos Van Dorn, peering out through the cracked glass of the wheelhouse with his binoculars.

'Engines one-third,' repeated Lomu, the first officer.

'Starboard two points.'

'Starboard two points, skipper,' the helmsman said, and spun the ship's wheel through a minor revolution. Van Dorn, an Afrikaner, was a self-taught sailor who still navigated by the old compass-point system rather than degrees. Each point on the compass was equivalent to about seven degrees. The helmsman had his eyes fixed on the binnacle as his hands shifted on the wheel.

'All stop,' Van Dorn said finally.

'All stop.'

'Drop anchor. Lomu, inform the boys that we're in position.'

'Aye, cap'n.'

The *Victoria* gradually lost way and came to a halt on the surface of the Great Lake. It was getting on for evening and the setting sun had filled the western sky with flame. Already, the stars were shining. On the shores of the lake the first fires had been lit and were lining the shore like beacons. The decks of the old steamer were in darkness, however, and crowds of men were milling about her decks while others hauled the towed canoes about her sides and dropped scramble nets down from the ship's rails.

Van Dorn walked out of the wheelhouse on to the wing-bridge to one side. He looked up at the grimy funnel to see the sparks and smoke that were still curling out of it.

'Bank her down,' he called back to the wheelhouse, and Lomu bent to blow breath into the old-fashioned speaking tube that connected the wheelhouse with the engine-room.

The *Victoria* had once been the *Tanganyika*. Built before the end of the First World War, she was a passenger steamer of close to five hundred tons and had served as a troop transport of sorts during that conflict. With the fall of the German colony, as Tanzania had been then, to the British at the close of the war, she had continued to serve her original mission of plying the waters of the lake, but under a more suitable name. Van Dorn had found her a rusting hulk, abandoned in a swamp west of Entebbe. Amazingly, her hull and boilers had still been sound, and all the rest was mere cosmetics. He had got her afloat within three months and placed her and her new captain at the disposal of the Ugandan Army. The Ugandans had seen his offer as an ideal opportunity to vent some of their spleen on their unfortunate neighbours without being seen to do so too blatantly, and so Van Dorn had acquired his crew of pirates, his 'boys', as he called them. Originally Bagandan privates in the national army, they had in time come to see themselves as his personal retinue, to be rewarded for their efforts with the loot of their nightly expeditions.

As for Van Dorn, not only did he receive all his expenses, plus a modest bonus from the Ugandan government – a government which was basically the military in another guise – he also had the pick of whatever loot his raiders managed to bring back from their nocturnal forays. And the girls who were part of that loot, they were sold up north through a series of Sudanese agents. Potentially, Van

Dorn thought, that was the most lucrative part of the whole operation. Whoever had thought slavery was dead in Africa was a fool, he concluded. It was still there, perhaps on a smaller scale than in the past; but as long as the demand existed, it would have to be satisfied. That was a fact of life.

Of course, if the Ugandan government knew that he was profiting in slavery, then his operation could well be shut down; even the genocidal senior officers of Idi Amin's army might draw the line at that. But when the projected invasion of Tanzania at last occurred – and from what Van Dorn could pick up in Kampala, it was not far away – then the potential for his lucrative little sideline would increase tenfold, such was the effect of war. He stood to make a tidy packet for himself if he could just keep the operation on course until the invasion was well underway.

But that led to the disquieting part, the one fly in his ointment – the reception that his boys had received on a raid less than two weeks ago.

Van Dorn had lost twenty-three men in that abortive raid, a fifth of his strength. And the boys had needed some very heavy persuasion to raid again. Of course, since then they had stayed away from the Mwanza area and had encountered no further problems, but still it made him uneasy. From the garbled reports his men had made that night, it seemed that the enemy, whoever they were, had been well armed, disciplined and mounted in fast-moving attack boats of some kind. Certainly not the profile of a Tanzanian force. Could there be foreign mercenaries working for Nyerere? If so, it was a worrying development, and one that the Ugandan authorities should really hear about. But if Van Dorn informed them of it they might either curb his raids, or worse, send army officers out as observers to keep an eye on things. He could not tolerate that, not at this stage. He'd just stick to the western shores of Victoria for a while.

The boys were struggling down the scramble nets now by the score, their weapons slung at their backs. There were splashes and curses as they fought to find their footing in the canoes below. Tonight they would be hitting a string of small villages south of Bukoba. Not so rich as the area around Mwanza, or as heavily populated, but a lot safer. It would be near here that the invasion would begin. Van Dorn guessed that the first Ugandan objective

78

would be the salient created by the meander of the Kagera, which lay between Lake Victoria and the rising highlands of Rwanda to the west. No harm, then, to soften up the area a little first in preparation for the T-55s of Idi Amin.

He peered over the side of the ship to where the canoes were now a mass of limbs and gun barrels. He looked at his watch, nodded to himself, then briefly flicked on the beam of a little torch at the assembled men below. A moment later came the soft splash of paddles, and the mass began breaking up as the canoeists started off on their way to the shore.

It was completely dark now – sunsets were brief in this part of the world, twilights non-existent – and Van Dorn could see the lights of the villages strung out like a series of glittering jewels on the horizon. Three miles away, far enough. He would wait a couple of hours, then light the masthead lamps to guide the canoeists back to the mother ship. For now it was just a question of waiting.

He yawned suddenly. This was the worst part. He had actually accompanied the boys on the first few raids, to get them into the swing of things, so to speak, but he was too old for that now. These pirates of his were for the most part in their late teens, impoverished members of the Baganda tribe who had joined the army as a way to get on the winning side and have some food to fill their bellies. Van Dorn sometimes felt a kind of paternal affection for them, but he knew that their lives would most likely be brief and violent. That was the way of things in this country, and had always been the way of things in Africa. Nothing had changed, except the methods of killing, and there was nothing anyone could ever do about it.

He yawned again, told Lomu to take over the watch, then went below to his cabin. Nothing interesting would happen now for hours. Best to get some sleep.

The plan, Willan thought, was a good one. The only problem was that it proceeded on a series of assumptions – or guesses, to put it crudely. If even one of those guesses proved to be wrong, then the whole thing would go for a ball of chalk, and his men might very well pay for it with their lives.

Twenty-four men in three Rigid Raiders, one of the Raiders trailing a pair of Kleppers. It had taken a lot of patching to get all three craft seaworthy for that night but so far they seemed to be holding up just fine.

Raider One carried the Command and Assault Group, consisting of Willan, Morgan, Prentiss and five trainee NCOs from the camp. Raider Two carried the Reconnaissance Group – Geary and Hill. Their canoes were towed behind them, bumping and jumping in the wake of the powerful outboards. Also on board were the rest of the Assault Group – Okello and five more of his Ugandans.

Raider Three carried the Interdiction Group. In it were Fraser, Gordon, Kigoma, and five more men – Tanzanians, these, as Kigoma had insisted.

Thanks to Prentiss, the mission was more heavily armed than it might have been. The bags he had brought with him on his flight turned out to contain two 7.62mm General Purpose Machine Guns, or 'Gimpies', and several hundred rounds of linked ammo. Raiders One and Three now had these weapons mounted in the prow of the boats.

Prentiss had not asked to come aong – he had just presented the weapons nonchalantly and seemingly assumed that he was included in the night's mission. There was also the fact that he had been a train fanatic in his youth, and knew all about handling a steam-driven engine. The knowledge had proved decisive, as he had probably known it would, Willan thought sourly. The MI6 agent was therefore included in the night's line-up, a line-up which had left two very bad-tempered SBS men, Breckenridge and Parker, cooling their heels back at camp. They had protested, but Willan had been adamant. He needed to leave somebody behind to keep an eye on things, and to continue the training if anything should go disastrously wrong.

It had taken them over six hours to cover the distance from Mwanza to their current location, for they had not wanted to use up too much fuel on the approach and had kept the speed down to less than twenty knots. Now they were cruising along at less than five knots, so that the usual roar of the outboards was down to a low purr. The three boats were at five-hundred-yard intervals, communicating by radio – which worked with eerie perfection over the flat surface of the lake – and keeping their eyes peeled for any sign of their objective.

This was the worst part, Willan thought to himself. They knew the approximate location of the target, but they could not be precise about it. She might be anywhere within twenty miles of them. They would simply quarter the lake, much as he and Prentiss had done in the aircraft that morning, until they found her. And hope that they were not spotted first. Like everything else in this country, the plan was to a certain extent dependent on a favourable set of tactical circumstances, otherwise known as luck.

'Romeo One, this is Romeo Three. Over.' It was Fraser's gruff voice coming over the headphones on 'whisper' mode. Willan thumbed the pressel switch and held the throat mikes of the 349 tighter to his Adam's apple.

'Three, this is One. Send. Over.'

'One, we see a light, I repeat, a light, at three o'clock off our axis, estimate within a thousand yards. Over.'

'All Romeo call-signs, this is Romeo One. Kill engines. I say again, kill engines.'

Within a few moments the engines of all three boats had died, and all they could hear was the splash and plop of waves and the cries of nocturnal birds out in the darkness.

'Got it,' Willan said, peering through the Individual Weapons Sight. The IWS was a long, heavy, metal sausage which looked like a swollen telescopic sight and was meant to sit on the breech of a rifle, but he was using it like a telescope now. It whined like a mosquito in his hands and turned the dark night into a landscape of bright flickering green. He could see Fraser's light now, a pinprick of white amid the green clutter in the sight, and a silhouette brighter than the cool night air about it – the warmth of a man-made object of some size floating on the surface of the lake.

'All call-signs, this is Romeo One. Objective in sight. Acknowledge. Over.'

'Romeo Three. Seen. Over.'

'Romeo Two. Seen. Over.'

So they had all now identified the target. What was in some respects the trickiest part of the mission was now over. They could go ahead with the plan.

'Romeo Two, this is One, launch Ducklings. Over.'

'Roger, out.'

Geary and Hill would be clambering into the Kleppers now, preparing to head out on a close-up 'eyeball' mission.

The two canoes moved along almost silently across the calm waters of the lake, the SBS men dipping their paddles carefully and economically. Sound travels far over water at night, like radio waves. They had no way of knowing how alert the crew of the steamer might be and so could take no chances.

It loomed above them now, a dark giant that blotted out the stars. They could see the dim glow of the binnacle in the wheelhouse, the crack of light from a badly drawn curtain over one of the portholes. The ship creaked and groaned slightly as she rode the slight swell, her anchor chain dipping and coming up out of the water again as her bow rose and fell.

The SBS men piloted their canoes to the very side of the ship, and there Geary found the scramble net. They paused a while, listening, then Geary tapped his comrade on the shoulder and pointed a finger skywards. A moment later he had hauled himself noiselessly out of the Klepper and was going up the side of the ship as smoothly as an ape.

Nothing.

He had the Ingrams cocked and ready. He padded across the deck, his rubber shoes making no sound, peering down hatches and into portholes.

Two men in the wheelhouse, one smoking, his cigarette a tiny red gleam. They seemed bored, listless. No problem.

He made his way aft. An open companion-way, the smell of old cooking and sweat. No lights down there. He started down the stairs into the pitch-blackness below.

No sounds . . . no . . . someone snoring. He continued aft below-decks like a dark ghost, and found himself in a larger hold-like space. Iron bunk-beds, all empty, a foul smell, a scatter of belongings. The place seemed utterly deserted. He left the way he had come, easing himself back into the canoe that Hill had held for him. And then the two men paddled back quietly to the waiting boats beyond.

'Romeo One, this is Duckling. Over.'

'Send. Over.'

'Operation complete. Two in wheelhouse, at least one below. No more that I could see. Over.'

'Roger. Wait, out.'

Excellent. So the pirates were still out on their little foray, and the ship had been left with a caretaker crew, no more. Willan took some moments to hone his plans, then said a few brief sentences over the radio. The plan was as simple and as clear-cut as he could have wished for. And now they were ready to put it into practice.

* * *

Lomu sucked on his cigarette moodily and stared out at the lights on the shore, watching and listening. When the first, faint sounds of gunfire came drifting across the lake he smiled broadly, as did the helmsman who shared the wheelhouse with him. The boys had gone in; they had started partying.

Even as he watched, he saw the fires on the coast grow and blossom, becoming miniature infernos as huts and *bomas* were put to the torch. He crushed out his cigarette and sighed. As Van Dorn's designated first officer, he did not get to join in the fun as often as he would have liked. But he was proud of his position. When the Afrikaner was off the ship, it was Lomu who was left in command. He had responsibilities that raised him above the teenage thugs who formed most of the ship's complement. And his share of the spoils was correspondingly larger, that was something.

He came from a lake-going race, being a native of the Ssese Islands to the south-west of Entebbe. From time immemorial his tribe, the Basese, had fished the lake and grown cassava and yams on their tiny islands. He had a wife and two children on Buggala, the largest of them. They were proud that their father had made a career in the army despite not being a member of the Baganda tribe, that he was second-in-command of a ship and rich as a king compared with the other islanders. He only wished that he could see them more often.

Was that a splash, out there on the water? Crocodile maybe, though they rarely came this far out from the coast. A bird perhaps. He stepped out of the wheelhouse.

Suddenly a dark shadow appeared out of nowhere. He had time to retreat a step, the cry frozen in his throat; then a hand was across his mouth and the knife slashed his jugular once, twice, and he was lowered twitching to the deck.

The helmsman had heard something. He leant out of the wheelhouse door, calling Lomu's name softly. The silenced 9mm rounds, fired as a pair of 'double-taps', blasted him back inside again and sprayed the interior of the wheelhouse with blood and viscera. One went clear through him and smashed the window behind, the sound of breaking glass shattering the quiet night wide open.

Willan paused a second, glaring at Prentiss, whose pistol was still smoking, the silencer doubling its length.

'I could have taken him!'

'Does it matter?' the Intelligence agent asked coolly.

Swearing under his breath, Willan thumbed the 349.

'All Romeos, go now, I say again, go now.'

At once, the deck of the old steamer came alive with figures, a band of shadows that moved quietly all over her. A group of them disappeared down the companionway. The only sound was the thump of feet on wood.

Willan examined the controls inside the wheelhouse, wiping blood off his hand.

'Can you really pilot this thing?'

Prentiss was examining them even more intently.

'Shouldn't be a problem. The gauges are the same as in a steam train. Pressure, temperature . . . Christ, this thing is a real antique.'

'As soon as we've cleared her, I want you down in the engine-room.'

'I'll need some stokers.'

'You'll have them.'

There was a shot, then a rattle of automatic fire from the bowels of the ship. Then silence.

'Two, this is One, send sitrep. Over.'

The reply took a moment to come. It was Geary, sounding out of breath.

'One, this is Two. Still clearing. One enemy down, no own casualties. Moving forward to the cabins.'

'Roger, out.'

Willan peered out of the shattered window of the wheelhouse.

'Romeo Three, this is One. Send sitrep. Over.'

Fraser's voice came next.

'One, we have flames on the shore and automatic weapon fire. Nothing on the lake itself so far. Over.'

'Roger, out.'

Fraser's boat was patrolling the waters between the *Victoria* and the shore in case any of the steamer's crew began returning early from their raid. If they did, they would have one hell of a hot reception. But Willan hoped that would not happen. He wanted this mission to be as simple and bloodless as possible.

Shouts from down below, and another series of shots. There were men all over the upper decks too; Kigoma and Okello's soldiers taking up fire positions all around the ship's rail. More of them were still waiting in the

Rigid Raiders below also, guarding the line of retreat.

Willan heard a loud splash, and there was another rattle of gunfire. He ran out of the wheelhouse, unable to sit still any longer. Suddenly all the men at the rail were firing madly at something in the dark water. The noise was deafening, and the muzzle flashes comprehensively destroyed Willan's night vision.

'Fuck! Cease fire! Cease fire!'

'A man jumped into the water!' It was Okello, wide-eyed and breathing fast. 'I think we got him.'

'Good. But from now on, fire only on my orders, OK, Okello?'

'Yes, Colonel.'

The Ugandan officer seemed put out. Too bad. There were few things more calculated to cause a 'blue on blue' than men firing wildly on full automatic at night. And besides, the muzzle flashes would be visible from the shore.

Geary and his team appeared out of the aft companionway.

'All clear, Sarge. One fucker got away. I think he was a white man. But from the sound of things, Kigoma's lot stitched him up pretty good. We now own a ship.'

'No problems?'

'One of Okello's lot got hit by a ricochet, but it's not serious. It all went like fucking clockwork.'

'Good news. Get lines down to the boats, Willy; I want them towed behind. We haven't the time to haul them up on deck. Get the rest of the men on board when you've done that, and send a detail of six down to the engine-room. We have to get this rust-bucket moving.'

'Aye aye, captain.' Willan could see Geary's grin as a white flash in his camouflaged face.

He rejoined Prentiss in the wheelhouse. The MI6 agent had hauled the bodies outside and was peering closely at the gauges that were on the bulkheads.

'They've banked the fires, probably trying to save fuel. We'll need to get the boilers stoked up and build up some steam before we can move.'

'How long will that take?'

'I don't know. I've never driven a steamship before.'

'Well, get to it. I've sent men down to the engine-room. We want to be out of here like yesterday.'

Prentiss left without another word. He seemed happy as a child at Christmas, while for

Willan the familiar feeling of disappointment was beginning to slide into place now that the excitement had peaked. He pressed the switch on the 349 again.

'Romeo Three, this is One, objective secure. Any sign of our friends? Over.'

'One, this is Three. There's a crowd on the beaches; we can see them backlit against the fires. I think our friends will soon be on their way back, over.'

Willan swore under his breath.

'OK, Three. If they put to sea before you hear from me again, you know what to do.'

'Roger, out.' Fraser's voice seemed to relish the prospect. His team had not yet fired their weapons in anger tonight.

It had all been very easy, Willan thought, easier than anything in that country had been so far. Well, that could change if Prentiss the steam-train enthusiast couldn't get this damn tub moving again.

He could hear the gunfire from the shore, carrying clearly over the water. The coastline was lit by a series of huge fires that gave the sky to the west an orange glow, like an early sunrise. He looked at his watch. It would be dawn in two hours, maybe less. By the time the sun came up he wanted to be as far away from here as possible. However good it might feel to be operating on water again, to be fighting the way he had been trained to fight, the truth was that they were intensely vulnerable out here. If one of Amin's MiGs happened by for any reason, they would be about as hard to take out as a large white, flightless duck. The thought did nothing to improve his temper.

Jock Fraser leaned on the bow of the Rigid Raider and trained the IWS on the brightly lit shore of the lake. Beside him, Gordon had the butt of the GPMG tucked into his shoulder and was peering intently over the sights. Kigoma was aft, his hand on the outboard control, waiting for a word. The other five soldiers had their AK47s trained on the shore as if they expected to open fire on it at any moment.

'Aye . . . aye.' Fraser squinted into the night-sight intently.

'No doubt about it, laddie: they're getting back in their wee canoes. I can see them pushing them out into the shallows. Aye . . . they're on their way.'

'Wish I had a night-sight for this fucker,' Gordon said, sighting down the long barrel of the GPMG. The linked bullets that fed the weapon were lolling over the bow of the boat like a glittering brass snake.

Fraser thumbed his 349. The throat mikes were digging into his throat but he ignored the discomfort.

'Romeo One, this is Three. Message. Over.'

'One, send. Over.'

'Our friends are putting out to sea. Estimate they will be at my location in figures fifteen. Over.'

'Roger. You know what to do. Good luck. Out.'

'So we're off and running then?' Gordon asked.

'Aye. Kigoma, get that motor going, will you? We're about to join the party.'

There was a roar as the outboard kicked in, and a moment later the bow of the boat rose as it foamed off towards the crowd of canoes that were beginning to leave the flame-lit shore.

'Well?' Willan asked impatiently.

'It's done,' Prentiss answered him. The MI6 agent was black with soot and coal dust, and sweat had carved white runnels down his face. He studied the dials and gauges in the wheelhouse intently.

'Yes, we're getting up a good head of steam now; the pressure is rising by the second. Okello has his men working like Trojans down in the engine-room; it's like a scene from Dante's Inferno down there.'

'So when . . . ?'

'One moment. There.' Prentiss straightened, smiling. 'We can start off any time you like, Sergeant.'

'Go to it then. Full bloody speed ahead.'

Prentiss yanked the old brass speed handle back and forward. There was the clanking of tinny-sounding bells. Then he opened up what looked to Willan like a throttle, and the ship quivered under their feet. There was the rumble of machinery, cogs turning, a thrum of power.

Willy Geary burst into the wheelhouse and yelled, 'We're moving!'

Prentiss took the ship's wheel and spun it to port. The deck canted a little under their feet as the old steamer picked up speed and came round in a sharp curve.

'Back the way we came, skipper?' Prentiss asked Willan ironically.

'Yes.' A moment later came the sound of sustained automatic fire from across the lake. Willan and Geary looked at each other. At almost the same moment the radio crackled into life in Willan's earphone.

'Romeo One, this is Three.' Fraser and his team, still out on the lake.

'One, send. Over.'

'Contact to the west of us. Our pirate buddies are out in force on the water. We're keeping their heads down. Any word on when to bug out? Over.'

'Romeo Three, hold them for figures ten, then make for the steamer. The masthead light is still on, and we've got her moving. Over.'

'Good news. Roger, out.'

'Things getting a little hot out on the water?' Prentiss asked.

'No more than we expected.' Willan found himself disliking the smug self-assurance of the Intelligence agent intensely. But there was no denying that without him the mission could not even have been mounted, much less become the success that it was.

The steamer churned on steadily. Morgan and Hill had thrown all the bodies overboard and were now going through the *Victoria*'s hold. Okello was supervising the engine-room crew.

'Dawn soon,' Geary said, sniffing the air like a hound. They could still hear the harsh bark of the GPMG out on the lake. But Jock could take care of himself.

The radio came to life again.

'One, this is Three. Breaking off contact now. Enemy paddling like hell back to shore. No own casualties. Over.'

'Nice one, Three. Rendezvous with mother ship ASAP, out.'

So that was that. Willan wondered if it was something about the country they were in and the way things happened, but he could have sworn that the cowboy attitudes of people like Prentiss were rubbing off on his men – and on himself for that matter. Take their voice procedure, for instance – it was all going to shit, becoming almost conversational. Could it be, he thought, that we're losing our edge? The success of the night's operation seemed to indicate otherwise, but he was still uneasy. The whole thing was like a *Boys' Own* adventure, complete with steamships and unruly natives. On the other side of the lake a genocidal regime was preparing to invade with tanks and jet aircraft. He mustn't lose sight of that.

'What are we going to do with this rustbucket now we've got her?' Geary asked curiously, breaking into Willan's thoughts.

'Do with her?'

'As Okello said: do unto others as they have bloody well done unto you,' Prentiss said firmly. 'Don't worry, chaps, we still have lots to do. This is only the opening skirmish.'

Willan and Geary shared a look of understanding. The war, if it could be called that, had indeed only just begun.

7

Major-General Isaac Lumago, Chief of Staff
of the Ugandan Army, sipped his tea and
stared across his desk at the scruffily dressed
Afrikaner. It had not been a good week.
Amin had just survived another assassination
attempt and had become even more distrustful
of his own top officers and civil servants.
There were rumours of rolling heads, and
when heads rolled in Uganda, they often did
so literally. Senior army officers who 'retired'
did so so completely that they were never
heard of again. To replace them, Amin usually
promoted nonentities from the ranks. Second
lieutenants became colonels overnight. Cap-
tains became brigadiers. And, inevitably, the
army suffered in terms of combat efficiency.

And now this. Lumago did not care for
mercenaries in general and for Loos Van Dorn
in particular, but orders had come down from

General Mustafa Adrisi, Defence Minister and deputy to Amin himself. This one was to be given a free rein against the Tanzanians. There were two reasons behind it, of course. One, so that he could be easily disowned if any outrage he perpetrated overstepped the mark, though in Amin's Uganda overstepping the mark with regard to brutality was not easy. And two, it was felt that Van Dorn would be more . . . creative if left to his own devices.

His usefulness, it seemed, had just about come to an end. He knew it, which was why he was sweating in the air-conditioned office, his eyes fixed on Lumago's face as though trying to read his own fate in the other man's features. Lumago liked that; it was good to show this bastard Afrikaner who had the power in this country.

'And you're sure they were white men, speaking English?' he demanded of Van Dorn.

'Yes, General. I heard them myself just before I jumped ship. There were blacks too – Bagandans, I'm sure of it. I heard the accents.'

'No names were mentioned?'

'No. It was a well-planned operation. We were caught completely by surprise.'

'Totally unexpected, eh?'

'Yes, General.'

'And yet less than a fortnight before your raiders were ambushed by what you call a similar force – well-armed, well-equipped, well-led.'

Van Dorn shifted uneasily in the chair.

'That is true.'

'And yet you kept this information to yourself. Why?'

'I . . . wanted to find out more about these men for myself. I could not come to you with mere rumours alone.'

'And yet these mere rumours have taken your ship and effectively destroyed your raiding forces. Our border patrols are picking up stragglers from the bush day by day. They had to fight their way back into Uganda. Over fifty are still unaccounted for, however.'

'Is there any way you can rescue them? Take a force in and get them out?'

Lumago stared at the Afrikaner coldly. 'They have no connection with the Ugandan government or military. They are pirates only, marauders owing allegiance to no one.'

'I see. I should have remembered.'

'You should.'

Lumago steepled his fingers and regarded the mercenary speculatively.

'And you have not answered my question satisfactorily. Why were we not informed that there were well-armed and well-trained white mercenaries operating out of Tanzania? That leads on to another, just as interesting, question. Why were you the only one of all your men to escape your ship?'

Van Dorn went pale under his tan.

'I told you, I jumped from a porthole when I heard the first shots, and swam to shore. Three bloody miles almost.'

'Have you had contacts with these soldiers of fortune?'

'Of course not.'

'You excuses are somewhat thin, Van Dorn. What if I were to tell you that I believe you to be lying, that I think you were in league with these men from the start and were allowed to escape by them because you are their . . . spy? Is that the right word?'

'If I was in league with them, then why come here? Why not stay in safety in Tanzania?'

'A good question.' Lumago raised his voice. 'Kinabau!'

A neatly uniformed soldier entered the room.

'Sir?'

'Have Mr Van Dorn escorted to the cells. See he is well treated. I shall want to talk to him again later.'

'Yes, sir.'

'Wait, damn it!' Van Dorn shouted, panic in his eyes now. 'I'm your ally; I'm telling you the truth!'

Lumago nodded at the soldier who had just entered. Kinabau slipped his .45 out of its holster and without warning clubbed Van Dorn on the side of his head. The Afrikaner staggered in his seat, then half rose. Kinabau pistol-whipped him again, this time across his face. Van Dorn fell to his knees. A third blow laid him unconscious on the floor, his breathing harsh and ragged through his broken nose.

Lumago nodded again, and Kinabau dragged the unconscious man from the room by his heels, thoughtfully shutting the door when they were both outside.

As Lumago leaned back in his chair he allowed himself a smile. Here was a morsel to offer up to Amin, a way of securing his own position in the purges to come. He had uncovered a Tanzanian spy, linked to white mercenaries. Heads would roll, all right, but his would not be one of them. Another storm weathered.

It would be easier when the war began, he thought. Things would loosen up. There was nothing like a war to improve the tone of an army, and to distract the heads of government from their navel-gazing. Well, it would not be long now.

He paused a second, then reached for a sheet of headed paper across his desk. He began writing a set of orders. This Tanzanian mercenary business had best be investigated.

8

The old steamer had made good time back to the camp, and they had anchored a hundred yards out from the beach in five fathoms of water. After that, the hard work had begun.

First, the unloading. It took most of a day, ferrying tons of equipment, supplies, weaponry and ammunition from the *Victoria* to the shore. Morgan, acting quartermaster for the camp, had rubbed his hands with glee at the sight of the stuff that was being ferried out from the old ship's bowels. Crates of AK47s, unopened and pristine. Ammunition, explosives, grenades, a dozen RPG7 rocket-launchers, a pair of Dragunov sniper rifles, boxes of Tokarev automatic pistols with hundreds of clips. The list was endless. He told Willan that they would be able to properly arm at least a third of the camp's recruits now. Two companies maybe. Okello and Kigoma were tasked to select the best of their soldiers and NCOs for the honour, and were nominated company commanders. It was, Willan reflected, like Christmas come early. Soldiers like nothing better than to be issued with mounds of brand-new equipment. Until they have to start cleaning it and carrying it around, that is.

But there were other things in the hold of the ship besides weaponry.

Down in the bilge, the lowest part of the hold, the enraged soldiers discovered fourteen young women, bound and gagged and laid in a row like sacks of flour. Three of them were already dead of dehydration, and the rest were dazed and mute, covered in bruises and all manner of filth. These were the merchandise that Van Dorn had been intending to sell up north to Sudan. Once again, Willan regretted that they had not bagged the Afrikaner on the night of the mission. He would have court-martialled him and then hung the bastard from the nearest tree.

The women were sent by truck to hospital in Mwanza, an escort of the most presentable of the recruits with them and Kigoma and Prentiss in the cab. Prentiss thought there might be some capital to be made out of their fate. Ugandan forces dabbling in slavery

– the headlines could be sensational. Willan saw them off with a distinct feeling of relief.

In addition to the unfortunate women, there were crates of much-appreciated supplies on board the ship. Tinned foods of every description, along with boxes of bananas, yams and plantains. The cornucopia eased the supply problem somewhat, and the success of the mission, both Kigoma and Prentiss had assured Willan, would engender swift reaction in Dar-es-Salaam. Willan did not intend to hold his breath. It was enough that he now had two fully equipped companies of soldiers who were well on the way to being adequately trained and whose morale was sky-high.

That still left some four hundred men for whom there were still not enough weapons, uniforms or sleeping-space, but it was best, Willan thought, not to look a gift-horse in the mouth.

As soon as the steamer was unloaded, he sent out Jock Fraser with a small team to reconnoitre a discreet little harbour for her. They found an overgrown cove half a mile from the camp, and after sweating over the boilers in the engine-room for a couple of hours, finally got the ship moved there and made sure she was thoroughly camouflaged.

A fire team of four men were on guard in her constantly; Willan had every intention of holding on to the old vessel, and he did not want the Ugandans either reclaiming or sinking her.

Two days passed, two of the busiest that Willan had yet spent in Africa.

The day after the taking of the steamer, three hundred more men appeared on the beaten earth of the parade ground. Rumours had been flying round the surrounding villages of a battle out on the lake in which the Ugandan raiders had been destroyed once and for all; and the villagers themselves had seen Willan's recruits with their brand-new weapons and equipment. Now more of them were keen to get in on the act.

It was impossible to house them and next to impossible to feed them, but the SBS did their best. The newest of the recruits were put under some of the better of the NCOs and turned their hands to constructing their own barracks. The forage parties began to be sent out again, and the cycle of training went on, slipping back into routine so quickly that at times Willan felt he had never soldiered anywhere else except Africa.

There were almost a thousand men in the

camp now, and it had been extended and
enlarged to nearly four times its original
size. Some of the most basic aspects of the
training could safely be left in the hands of
the new NCOs, but most was still handled
by the eight-man SBS section. The men
found themselves getting up before dawn
and getting to bed well after last light. They
were continually tired, and had begun to pick
up some of the more unpleasant inhabitants
of the bush, such as bush lice and ticks. Tony
Parker, nominated the post's medical officer
because he had completed a field medics'
course before leaving England, had his hands
full with training injuries, continual delousing
and three suspected cases of malaria, as well
as having to oversee the diet of the men to
make sure it was adequate.

'We're running on a shagging shoestring,'
Geary said one evening while seated at one
of the cooking fires.

'You can't train up an army like this – not
in the long term. We have two companies
of good men, bombed up to the nines.
But the rest are glorified boy scouts with
nothing but *pangas* and their grandfathers'
shotguns. It's a farce. We can't even stock-
pile food.'

'Hand to mouth,' Jock Fraser agreed, nodding. There were dark rings under his eyes that the flames of the fire seemed to make deeper.

Willan was irritated, annoyed. They were only voicing his own views but he was not in the mood for it right now.

'We'll see what Kigoma and Prentiss bring back from town. If they can guarantee that we'll receive proper support from the government, then our worries are over. If not . . .'

'If not?' Fraser asked.

'Then we'll have to scale down the operation. We're running an overstrength battalion on the resources of a large company. It can't go on.'

'What about other ops? Any word?' Breckenridge asked. The fittest of the SBS men, he was now beginning to look gaunt and worn because he had the least excess flesh to draw upon.

'Not a whisper,' Willan answered him wearily. 'But like I said, we'll have to wait on that until Prentiss gets back from Mwanza.'

'Whenever that is,' Geary muttered.

It was not as long as they thought it might be. A week after the arrival of the new recruits word was brought to Willan of a convoy moving up

the Mwanza road towards the camp. He took
out a section of soldiers to meet it at the gate.
The plume of dust the vehicles sent up into
the air was visible for miles. He and Morgan,
who had joined him by the gate sentry's hut,
exchanged glances.

The line of vehicles ground to a halt in
front of the gate, and Kigoma jumped out
of the lead truck, grinning and saluting
flamboyantly.

What the fuck? Willan wondered.

There were at least a dozen vehicles
in the convoy. Most of them were the
inevitable Second World War trucks, but
there were also a trio of M3 half-tracks
bristling with fifty-calibre heavy machine-
guns. Perched atop one of the half-tracks
was a woman in khaki fatigues hung about
with bags and sporting a camera with
a telephoto lens. She was enthusiastically
clicking off photographs of the camp and
the vehicles.

Prentiss jumped out of the lead truck. Like
Kigoma, he was grinning broadly.

'What the hell is going on – and who the
fuck is that?' Willan demanded, pointing at
the photographer.

'That's the press, my dear fellow,' Prentiss

told him, unabashed. 'And we have come bearing the greetings of the Tanzanian government, and a load of gear to go with them.'

Willan paused a moment, considering.

'Kigoma, Prentiss – the HQ hut, if you please. Morgan, get that bloody woman out of the way somewhere, and stop her taking those bloody photos.'

'Pleasure, Sarge,' Morgan said, grinning evilly.

'What's going on?' Willan asked, once he, Kigoma and Prentiss were alone in what he called his office: a small, mud-walled room in the headquarters hut.

'Equipment, Colonel,' Kigoma answered him, plainly surprised by Willan's attitude. 'The government has opened one of the arsenals in Mwanza and let us take what we need from it.'

'And they've promised to set up a proper supply line,' Prentiss added. 'From now on you'll have truckloads of food and other gear every day.'

'Why?'

'Isn't that what you were hoping for?'

'Yes. But why the sudden cooperation, the

recognition of our existence – and why the photographer?'

Prentiss looked distinctly coy.

'Well, you could say that the Tanzanian government, or rather Julius Nyerere, has come to a little accommodation with us. The idea is that they will supply this camp and recognize it as an official training camp of the Tanzanian National Army.'

'But most of the recruits are Ugandan exiles – like Okello.'

'Yes, but we'll keep that under our hat, shall we? And we'll also keep it quiet that there are British nationals organizing and running the training. As far as the country and the rest of the world is concerned, this is a wholly Tanzanian set-up.'

Willan looked at Kigoma. 'And who is to be commanding officer?'

Kigoma nodded. 'I am, Colonel.'

'I thought as much. What about my men – and Okello?'

'They'll keep doing the jobs they've been doing up until now,' Prentiss said smoothly. 'But they'll be discreet about it, that's all.'

'Discreet! Is that why the photographer is here? To keep things discreet?'

'In a way, yes. She's been well briefed by the

Tanzanian Foreign Ministry. She'll take photos of Tanzanian soldiers undergoing training and of the camp in general. These photos will be circulated to prove to Uganda that Tanzania has an army of sorts and does not intend to take lightly any aggression on the part of Amin.'

Willan sat down in his wicker chair, shaking his head.

'A bloody PR exercise – is that all this is?'

'By no means,' Prentiss told him sharply. 'These men you are training are the only organized force capable of offering the Ugandan Army real resistance, should it choose to invade. The rest of the Tanzanian forces are little more than untrained militias, armed with tribal weapons and old hunting rifles. No, Willan, these recruits of yours are going to be trained to perfection, and then shipped up north to the Kagera salient.'

'A deterrent, or a sacrifice?'

'They'll try and halt Amin in his tracks long enough for the delay to prove fatal to his regime. He is already tottering, or else he wouldn't be considering an invasion in the first place.'

'I've got a thousand men here. Do you really think that'll be enough?'

'It'll have to be. You've got a month to

finish licking them into shape; then they're all heading north to dig in north of the River Kagera.'

Willan digested this for a second, frowning. There was a babble of activity outside as the convoy of trucks and armoured vehicles were unloaded. He heard a woman's voice raised in outrage but it barely registered in his mind.

'I see. They'll still be pretty raw after a month, but I guess needs must when the devil drives. What about Okello? I take it he'll keep his command.'

'None of the command positions are to be changed, Colonel,' Kigoma said. He had bought himself a new uniform, Willan noticed, and sported a .45 automatic in a webbing holster, much as Okello did.

Willan raised both hands. 'All right then, tell me what you've brought.'

There was a fresh commotion outside that interrupted Prentiss's reply. The sound of flesh being struck, and then the unmistakable sound of Morgan's voice raised in startled fury. A moment later a tall, blonde apparition with blazing eyes threw open the door to Willan's office and stormed in with Morgan in hot pursuit.

'What the hell's going on here?' the woman demanded in an Australian accent.

Willan looked coldly at her a second, then addressed the purple-faced Morgan.

'Talk fast.'

'I tried to take her camera away, sir, like you said, but she wasn't having it. Clocked me one in the eye.'

The photographer was still clutching her precious camera in one hand, Willan noted. Still ignoring her, he turned to Prentiss, who was smiling behind his hand.

'You say this woman had been briefed by the Tanzanian Foreign Ministry?'

'Oh yes. She's doing us a favour really. Don't worry; she knows what to snap and what not to.'

Willan nodded curtly, then said to Morgan, 'That'll be all, QM. You might want to see the MO about your bruises.'

Morgan gave Willan a glare, then stomped out. The photographer was standing there taking it all in, her bosom heaving very prettily, Willan could not help but notice. He dragged his eyes off it to her face.

'My apologies, miss, for any inconvenience. You arrived at a rather hectic time.' Spoken like a true CO, he thought.

The young woman – she couldn't have been out of her twenties – threw back her hair with one hand.

'Doesn't a gentleman and an officer stand when a lady enters a room?' she asked archly.

'Doesn't a lady knock before she enters?' Willan retorted. 'Now, if you'll excuse us, we have a lot to discuss. Go and take your pictures. You won't be molested again.'

'I'd rather sit in on your meeting if you don't mind,' she said.

'I do mind. If you'll excuse us.' Willan stood up, closely followed by Prentiss and Kigoma.

The photographer looked at the trio for a moment, then turned and stormed out again without another word.

'Spirited creature,' Prentiss said appreciatively.

Willan was still thinking of the way her buttocks had filled the khaki trousers. It had been a long time since he had seen a sight like that. He shook his head as if to clear it and took his seat once more.

'She's trouble. She's so much trouble I can smell it.'

'She's only here to take a few photos, Willan. Don't get paranoid on me.'

'Paranoia has kept me alive before now.'

'You've been working too hard – all of you. How about a bit of R and R?'

'What do you mean?'

'Beers, Willan. A relaxing evening. Civilized surroundings. Have you forgotten what it's like to wear civvies for a while?'

The thought was appealing, Willan thought. He was starting to shake his head, though, when Kigoma spoke.

'All the men from the first batch of recruits need some time off, Colonel. I think it would be a good idea to give them two days to see their families.'

'But will they come back again once we let them go?' Willan asked.

'I don't doubt it, sir.'

Willan thought again of that khaki-clad backside, and then of a long, cold beer. He blinked, almost tasting it.

'Let's get done here with the paperwork,' he said. 'Then we'll see about a forty-eight-hour pass perhaps.'

'Excellent,' Prentiss said. 'I may even be able to lend you some presentable clothes.'

It would be good, Willan admitted to himself. All the men needed a break. He had a feeling that it would be the last one they had for a very long time.

Prentiss's idea of presentable clothes, Willan thought sourly, did not quite mesh with his own. He had been given a pair of flared white trousers, white socks, white shoes which pinched his feet cruelly and a Bermuda shirt which was louder than the music currently grating over the tinny loudspeakers in the bar.

They were in the Deluxe Hotel in Mwanza, off Uhuru Street. The best place in town, Prentiss had informed them authoritatively. Well, it was air-conditioned, which raised goose-bumps on their arms after so long in the oven-hot bush, and the Tusker beer was cold, which hurt their throats but was very welcome. They sat at the bar in their borrowed clothes and raised the frosted bottles to their lips in appreciative silence. Cold beer, one of the small but important pleasures in life.

There were six of them. Willan, Breckenridge, Jock Fraser and Gordon comprised the SBS contingent, and alongside them were Okello, looking incredibly neat as always in

120

pressed shirt and chinos, and Prentiss, doing his Man from Havana impersonation again and smoking hideous local cigarettes. Somehow or other, the MI6 agent had got hold of civilian clothes for all of them, though they were garish, mismatched and ill-fitting in the extreme. Perhaps the bastard had done it on purpose, Willan thought. But he didn't much care. It was enough, for now, to be cool and clean and drinking beer in civilized surroundings – all on Prentiss's expense account. Now there was a laugh.

'I'm going to have another shower,' Breckenridge said, getting up from his stool.

'Another one?' Gordon protested. 'Man, you'll wash yourself down the plughole if you keep that up.' It was Breckenridge's third of the day.

'Making up for lost time. See you later, lads.' He wandered off to his room, a little unsteadily.

'If only Mick could taste this,' Jock Fraser said, eyeing his beer blissfully.

'Poor bastard is probably up to his armpits in gun grease,' Gordon grinned. Willan shot him a warning glance, and he sobered. If anyone asked, they were businessmen, out here for a little aerial safari with Prentiss's cover company. The other four SBS men were back at camp, as Gordon had said, up to their armpits in work with Morgan. As QM, Morgan was still sorting and storing and redistributing the tons of equipment and weapons that had arrived the day before. Geary and Hill were breaking in the latest batch of recruits, and Parker was dealing with a mild epidemic of dysentery which had hit the camp only in the last day. Worse luck for him. But they would all get their turn at the fleshpots of Mwanza, if there were any. Mwanza was an attractive little town, the terminus of the Dar-es-Salaam railway and a port on Lake Victoria which handled large quantities of cotton, tea and coffee. It was surrounded by hills which still looked fairly green despite the heat of the dry season, but it was not exactly a cosmopolitan place.

The bar of the hotel they were in was bland enough, only the stuffed animals' heads on the walls giving any clue to the continent they were in. All the SBS men had an adequate supply of Tanzanian shillings, and Prentiss had made it clear that money was no object. They were to have as good a time as they possibly could. Willan wondered if the Intelligence agent knew something he was not telling them. The whole thing was a little like the condemned man's last meal, and that thought made him suspicious and uneasy.

He was already a little drunk, which irritated him. He seemed to have lost his head for alcohol in the dry days in the bush. He'd have to be careful.

'Well, Gordy,' Fraser said, draining his glass flamboyantly. 'Time to hit the town before it hits us.'

'Coming, boss?' Gordon asked Willan.

'No, you go ahead. And mind your Ps and Qs, you hear me?'

'Aye aye. Come on, Okello – you want to show us where the action is?'

Fraser, Gordon and Okello left the bar, obviously girding their loins for a night of town-painting. Willan was not in the mood somehow. He sat beside Prentiss and breathed in the other man's foul cigarette smoke. When Prentiss offered him one wordlessly, he took it.

'Christ!' he spluttered, his first drag making his head swim. 'What are these made of – camel shit?'

'They take a little getting used to,' Prentiss answered imperturbably.

They ordered more beers. Willan lowered his

voice, even though the bar was almost deserted and the barman was cleaning glasses listlessly at the other end of the room.

'Spit it out, man,' he said. 'You're holding out on us. You know something we don't.'

Prentiss raised an eyebrow. 'Oh, I do, do I?'

'Damn straight.'

The other man drained the beer in his bottle and blew out another cloud of evil-smelling smoke.

'The war is on,' he said at last quietly.

'When?'

'Ah, now there's a question. We think in about a month's time – the end of October.'

'How do you know?'

'Sources in Kampala who have managed to avoid the butcher's knife. You're going to have one hell of a fight on your hands, Willan.'

'Tell me about it. Is that why the Tanzanian government has suddenly become so cooperative?'

Prentiss nodded. 'If you had a TV at the camp you'd have been able to see the way Amin and Nyerere have been mouthing off at one another. They really hate each other personally. The grapevine in government circles here has it that there's been a change of plan.'

'What do you mean?'

'The original stategy was simply to defend Tanzania from attack – which is where you came in. But increasingly the feeling seems to be that if we can halt the Ugandan Army, that's no longer enough. We have to push it back and invade in turn.'

Willan laughed shortly. 'You can't be serious.'

'Oh, but I am. There are militias being raised all over the country. Nyerere is mightily determined.'

'Jesus. Well, our mission was to train up a defence force – no more.'

'Your mission, Sergeant,' Prentiss told him acidly, 'is to obey orders.'

'So that's what all this is about – giving the men a final fling before night falls.'

'Yes.'

Willan became silent. His suspicions had been correct. His team were nothing but pawns in a larger game, pieces which would be sacrificed without question if that was what it took to win the game.

'You bastard,' he hissed. 'You had an idea of this all along. You knew that we weren't just going to be a training team. We're to be little better than mercenaries, doing our employer's bidding.'

'You are carrying out the wishes of Her Majesty's Government,' Prentiss told him calmly. 'Whitehall concurs with my recommendations and has put you at Nyerere's disposal.'

'Nyerere is happy to use us, but he won't acknowledge our existence.'

'Of course. Don't be naive, Willan. And don't drink so quickly.'

'Oh, fuck off,' Willan said, feeling suddenly tired.

'As I think you said once before, you do what you are paid to do. In your line of work you can expect nothing more.'

'Except a nameless grave perhaps.' Prentiss was right: he was a little drunk. He had best watch himself, he thought, and stood up.

'I think I'll go and seek out some more congenial company.'

'As you wish. But remember who you are supposed to be. And don't get laid, Willan. The whores in this part of the world have diseases you wouldn't believe.'

Willan left the bar without another word.

He wandered down the street in the waning sunlight. It was getting on towards evening and the streets were crowded with taxi-vans, donkeys pulling huge carts, women with their burdens balanced impossibly on their heads. The pavements were choked by street stalls selling every manner of fruit and vegetable that Willan had ever seen, and many he had not. He found himself a little open-air watering-hole along the Makongoro road, and sat there with a warm beer in his fist, watching the rowdy, colourful life of the town wind down into the humid night.

The Simba Mechanized Regiment was one of the best formations in the Ugandan Army. It was stationed along the border between Uganda and Tanzania and had its headquarters in the town of Mbarara. Its commander, Lieutenant-Colonel Kasese, studied the hand-delivered and handwritten orders he had just received from Kampala, and frowned. He had heard rumours, of course; they had been flying around for days. But this was the first time that the chain of command had taken any notice of them. His men had picked up a dozen stragglers from Van Dorn's shattered raiders, who gabbled about white water-borne mercenaries who had ambushed them on the lake and who had a training camp near Mwanza. Now it seemed that Kampala wanted these rumours verified, and his men were to do it.

'Orderly!' Kasese barked. He was an old soldier, a veteran of the pre-Independence army and entirely loyal to his superiors, even though he knew of and detested the excesses of the regime they supported. It was one of the reasons he had been given this important command.

'Sir?' the orderly asked, entering the little office.

'Get me Ngoro, the pilot officer, and ask Lieutenant Oyite to step in also.'

There were a trio of French-built Puma helicopters based at Mbarara. If the Chief of Staff wanted him to reconnoitre this reported camp, then he would do it. But he also decided that if he found it, he would order his men to do more than just look at the place. He'd give these mercenaries a taste of their own medicine.

Willan drank more beer, now feeling distinctly fuzzy-headed. By this time it was dark, and he was beginning to wonder if he could remember the way back to the hotel. He rubbed the sweat from his face and swatted a buzzing fly that wanted to crawl into the neck of his bottle.

'Buy you a beer?'

He looked up, startled. It was the Aussie photographer. How the hell had she got here? But he found that he didn't much mind. He drained the last gurgle of warm liquid in his bottle.

'Sure.'

She sat beside him without further invitation and ordered two beers. Willan looked at her narrowly. No camera in evidence this time, but an ankle-length skirt with a thin blouse. He could see the imprint of her nipples in the light material.

'Cheers,' she said, and clinked bottles with him.

He swallowed, trying to blink his brain clear.

'What do you want?' he asked.

'Charming. You'll go far with chat-up lines like that.'

Willan sighed. 'I'm in a non-charming line of work, and you're a photographer . . .'

'Photojournalist.'

'Whatever. And I have to be suspicious. All right?'

She nodded. 'All right. Listen, I wanted to

apologize for what happened yesterday: me barging in like that. I understand that you're under a lot of pressure at the moment, you and your men.'

'Apology accepted,' Willan said in a neutral voice, still deeply suspicious. He might be drunk, but he wasn't stupid.

'How did you find me?' he asked.

'This isn't a big town. Prentiss said you'd wandered off like you wanted to be on your own, so I thought you'd avoid the glitzier hotels and such.'

'All two of them.'

She laughed. 'Yeah. So here I am.'

'Just to apologize.'

'Maybe.'

'Bullshit.'

'My, you really do know how to treat a girl.'

'To me you're not a girl, you're a snoop.'

'That's a pity.'

Willan laughed. 'Who are you anyway? Mata Hari?'

She stuck out a hand in a very masculine manner. 'Sue Morris,' she said.

Willan took it. 'John Willan. Enchanted.'

'You don't look it.'

'That's the kind of guy I am. You're not

going to get a story out of me if that's what you're thinking.'

She paused, and then the flirtatious manner disappeared completely.

'All right, you bastard, so I'm here to sniff after a story. That's my job. And there *is* a story here, somewhere – a big one. What the hell are a bunch of British soldiers doing running a camp in Tanzania in the first place? And that guy Prentiss, he's . . .'

'I know. A spook.'

'Yeah. And the Tanzanian Foreign Ministry have been trying to get their hands on my films. It's like they're putting together some sort of propaganda exercise. And then all this crap on TV with Nyerere and Amin slagging each other off. What the hell's going on?'

'I've been asking that question myself ever since I arrived in this country,' Willan said mildly.

'Is it war? Is there going to be a war?'

Willan looked at her carefully. 'Can I go off the record?'

'Sure.'

'Then yes, there's going to be a war, very soon.'

'So that's why you're here.'

'That's right, sweetheart. Me and my lads

are the knights in shining armour who're going to help deliver the country from the paws of Amin's thugs. That's the theory anyway.'

She was visibly excited now. 'What a story this'll make!'

'That was off the record,' Willan warned her quickly.

'Yes, yes, of course. But now that I know what's going to happen, I'll know the right places to start digging. Thanks, Willan.' She raised her beer bottle to him.

'I don't suppose you'd consider leaving the country. Things are going to get very hot and sticky when Amin's tanks roll across the border.'

'Not on your life.'

'I thought so.'

'So you Poms have been brought in to beef up the local defenders, eh? That means you'll be in the thick of it when the shit hits the fan.'

'It's what we're paid for,' Willan said curtly, remembering Prentiss's words.

'I guess. You poor bastards.' She laid a hand on his arm. Willan was not sure if her sympathy was genuine or if she was just trying to soften him up. Either way, he didn't mind. He had not had a drink with a pretty woman in an awfully long time, though he could have done without all the verbal sparring.

'You look as though you could do with a square meal and a good night's sleep,' Sue said. 'Don't you eat when you're out in the bush?'

'Sure. Antelope and caterpillars.'

'How long are you in town for?'

'One night only, sweetheart. It's a flying visit. Tomorrow evening we head back out into the *ulu*.'

She stood up, and tugged him to his feet.

'We'd best make the most of it then. Come on, I'll take you to a much nicer place.'

'What are you going to do: take advantage of me? Maybe I'm not that kind of guy.'

'I think you are. Come on.'

Willan let himself be led away. He liked the way she held his arm.

It's all a big show, he told himself. She's just after information.

But at that moment, he really didn't give a shit.

9

The helicopters came in low, just after dawn. Those men who were still in camp had just assembled on the parade ground when the flight of three Pumas burst into view, so near the ground that they sent up clouds of choking dust from the dry clay below.

'Whose the hell are they?' Willy Geary yelled, running through the thick dust and cocking his AK47 at the same time.

The answer came in the form of a bright flare of automatic fire from the open side door of the lead chopper. The gunner strafed the packed parade ground, sending men screaming and toppling into the dirt.

'Take cover!' Mick Morgan was shouting. 'Get off the fucking square!'

The three helicopters circled the camp in dizzying swoops, barely a hundred feet off the ground, and from the sides of all three came jets of yellow flame as the door gunners let rip. The new recruits, most of whom had been at the camp for less than two days, ran panic-stricken in all directions. The choppers herded them like sheep and cut them down with hundreds of rounds of machine-gun fire. Geary and Morgan were out in the square with the crowds of terrified recruits, kicking, shoving and cursing them into the shelter of the huts. At the same time, Parker and three of the more experienced of the NCOs were manning two GPMGs, two firing the machine-guns while two provided living rests for the weapons by crouching with the barrels on their shoulders.

Tracer bounced about the camp, raining down from the swirling choppers and arcing up from the two machine-guns on the ground. There was a louder explosion and a flare of red light, and an RPG7 round, fired by Hill, streaked off into the sky. It exploded against the tail rotor of one Puma and the helicopter began to spin in lazy circles, out of control. The fuel caught just before it hit the ground and it exploded in a huge fireball, obliterating the HQ hut.

More fire was exchanged, but the helicopter pilots had had enough. They banked steeply, the door gunners still blazing away at the camp buildings, then headed out across the lake while a last RPG round fired by Hill fell short and sent up a geyser of foam in the water below them. Then they were gone, roaring off northwards.

The camp was on fire, the tracer rounds having set light to the dry brush that formed the roofs of the buildings. There were bodies everywhere, and amid thick clouds of obscuring dust, men still screaming in agony.

The SBS men dropped their weapons and began organizing firefighting teams, forming a human chain of men down to the lake and passing buckets of water up from the shore by hand. Blazing thatch was torn down, precious stores were carried out of blazing buildings and the human water-chain worked incessantly, ignoring the cries of the wounded. But the wind picked up and began fanning the blaze. They gave up fighting the fires and instead began salvaging what they could from the buildings before they were consumed. The wounded were dragged away to receive crude first aid. Trucks were backed into the camp to help with the evacuation. Exploding ammunition sent red-hot metal careering across the camp, wounding more men. The burning buildings sent a tower of smoke up into the clear morning sky that could be seen for miles.

Willan opened his eyes. They felt as though they were full of hot sand, and his mouth tasted as though a monkey had taken a dump in it. He groaned and turned over. Into the face of Sue. She was fast asleep, snoring slightly, her cheek pillowed on the back of one hand.

Willan blinked. For a moment he was entirely bewildered. He sneaked a look under the sheet that covered them both and saw her long, tanned body, naked as the day she was born. He whistled softly at the sight, some of the events of the preceding night coming back to him.

I'll be damned, he thought. I'll be damned. His brown face broke into a grin. A moment later his splitting headache made it vanish.

He sat up. They were in his hotel room and their clothes formed an ungainly puddle at the foot of the bed. Beer bottles everywhere; they had made use of room service well into the early hours.

He could hear the street noise already, and squinted at his watch. God, it was only five o'clock. No wonder he still felt drunk. He lay back on the bed and silently studied the features of his sleeping companion.

There was a sudden hammering on the door that brought him bolt upright in the bed and made Sue murmur and shift sleepily.

'Willan! Wake up! Open the door!' It was Prentiss's voice. Strange to hear the MI6 so agitated.

Willan grabbed the sheet, wrapped it about himself and shambled to the door. He opened it, forgetting about the uncovered girl on the bed behind him.

Prentiss's face was unshaven, and the blast of early-morning breath that came from it made Willan wince.

'What the hell do you want?'

'The camp, Willan,' the other man hissed. 'The camp has been attacked.'

'*What?*'

'Willan?' Sue's voice came from the bed. 'What are you doing?'

'What do we know?' Willan asked Prentiss, cursing his muddled head.

'Choppers, just after dawn. They shot the place up, and there's been a fire. We've got a truck waiting.'

'I'll get dressed.'

He turned to find Sue glaring at him and

trying ineffectually to cover herself with her hands. 'What the hell's going on?' she asked.

Willan threw the sheet at her and grabbed his trousers.

'Sorry, kiddo. Duty calls. I have to run.'

'Where are you going? You can't just . . .'

But Willan and Prentiss were already out of the door, sprinting down the hotel corridor, the SBS man buckling his belt as he ran.

'Jesus,' Willan said. 'What a shambles.'

'It spread too fast, what with the wind off the lake,' Geary explained. 'The buildings went up like bonfires.'

The camp was little more than a square of blackened shells. Smoke still trickled from the burnt-out buildings and the remains of the helicopter were scattered everywhere, ragged shards of blackened metal. The place stank.

'What about casualties?' Willan asked.

Geary wiped his brow. He was black with soot and ash and the sweat was cutting pale streaks down his face.

'Fourteen dead, twenty-nine wounded. Of the wounded, at least twenty are never going to be any use to us again. They've been shipped to Mwanza. I have burial details at work as we speak, though Kigoma reckons that some of the families will want the bodies to dispose of themselves.'

'Best make it quick then. We don't want dead bodies lying around in this heat. What about equipment?'

I'd say we saved about two-thirds of it. We lost a lot of ammo, and nearly all the stores, but we got the weapons away all right.'

'How are we for ammo then?'

Geary shrugged apologetically. 'Sorry, Sarge, no idea. It's been chaos here all day.'

Willan nodded grimly. 'Of course. I'll get Morgan on to it.'

'Sarge, I'm sorry. I wish I could have thought of something . . .'

'Don't blame yourself, Willy. You did all you could. At least you shot down one of the bastards. That may make them think twice before they try anything like this again.'

'That was Hill, with an RPG no less. Bloody lovely shot.'

There was a loud, echoing rumble off in the sky that seemed to roll from horizon to horizon. Willan raised his head and studied the heavy clouds that had been obscuring more and more of the sky even as they spoke.

'If I didn't know any better, I'd say it was about to rain.'

'They've been building up all day. Any fresh orders, Sarge?'

'Keep the men at the clean-up, and have all the salvaged equipment stockpiled near the trucks. How are we for petrol?' The camp's petrol supply had been stored a few hundred yards away in a camouflaged dump in the bush.

'Tons of the stuff. Thank Christ we didn't set the dump nearer the camp.'

'Amen.' Willan looked at his watch. 'Are any of the buildings still habitable?'

'One of the long sleeping huts still has a bit of roof at one end.'

'Right. O-Group there in one hour. We have to put our heads together and figure out what the hell to do next. Tell the others. I want Jock and Morgan there.'

'Right, Sarge.' Geary marched off.

More thunder. The clouds were darkening by the minute. Willan didn't like the look of them at all.

An hour later, Willan had finally rid himself of the ridiculous civvies that Prentiss had obtained for him and was back in uniform again. He sat on a rough bunk-bed in the only building of the camp which still had a fragment of a roof and most of its walls. Around him sat or squatted Geary, Morgan, Fraser, Prentiss, Kigoma and Okello. Everyone had a notebook open and ready, except Prentiss, who smoked cigarette after cigarette.

'First things first,' Willan said. 'Adjutant Geary, what's the situation with regard to the men?'

'We have 740 men in camp at the moment who have had some rudimentary training,' Geary told him, reading figures from his notebook. 'Of those 740, perhaps three hundred are well enough trained to be front-line troops – the two companies of Okello and Kigoma here. They're nearly all Ugandan exiles. These two companies are well equipped. As for the rest, they're a little raw, and we're short over a hundred weapons. The three hundred – less now – new recruits who arrived in the last couple of days have done virtually nothing at all. They are untrained and totally without equipment.'

Willan nodded. 'So, two strong companies and another three weak ones. What about equipment, QM?'

Morgan cleared his throat. He was looking a little the worse for wear.

'We've lost three-quarters of our food stores,

just under half our ammunition, all our bedding and spare uniforms, and thirty-six rifles which we couldn't get out of the armoury in time.'

'How many rounds per man do we have?' Willan asked.

Morgan scribbled in his notebook for a second.

'About six mags per head – 180 rounds. Plus RPG rounds – plenty of those – and some two thousand link for the GPMGs.'

'So we can fight a battle, but not a war,' Willan said.

'Right. And it had better not be a long battle.'

'All the vehicles OK?'

'Yes, no problem there. But we've only a thousand rounds for the three Brownings on the M3s. The rest went up in the fire.'

Willan cursed softly but viciously for a second. Then he turned to Prentiss and Kigoma.

'Right, what's the chance of resupply from Mwanza in the very near future?'

Kigoma looked at the ground. Prentiss stared at the glowing tip of his cigarette.

'Mwanza is cleaned out,' the Intelligence agent said quietly. 'We may be able to get something from Dodoma, I'm not sure. If we can't, then it'll have to come from Dar-es-Salaam.'

'Ten days to get here, minimum,' Morgan said in disgust. 'Are you saying we can expect nothing?'

'Very little. For a couple of weeks, at least, we'll just have to get by on what we've got.'

There was a great tearing roar of thunder which appeared to erupt right overhead. It seemed to have grown very dark outside.

'Is it my imagination, or is there a fuck of a storm brewing?' Morgan asked.

'The rains. I think they may be coming early,' Okello said. He was still in his smart civilian clothes but they were grimed with soot.

'Terrific. We have almost a thousand men with no roof over their heads,' Willan growled. 'Things just get better and better.'

'Might I make a suggestion?' Prentiss asked.

'Go ahead.'

'We knew that we were due to move up to the Kagera salient within a month anyway. I suggest that we make the move at once and get the men dug in – especially if the rains are indeed coming early. There's not a lot we can do here in a month. We certainly can't rebuild the camp.'

'What about the new recruits?' Geary asked. 'They've had no training whatever.'

'Discharge them,' Prentiss said promptly. 'We've no weapons or uniforms for them, and we no longer have the facilities to train them. They're just more mouths to feed.'

Kigoma and Okello started to protest at this, but Willan held up a hand. He had to wait for another peal of thunder to pass before speaking. As he did, lightning flashed outside.

'Prentiss may be right. We must cut our losses. It'll be hard enough looking after the men we have. As I see it, we have five companies of effectives: a good-sized battalion. We'll take it north and dig in. If nothing else, we can give anything that meets us a very bloody nose. Kigoma, will your superiors approve an early move north?'

Kigoma looked sullen, but after a moment he nodded reluctantly. 'The Ugandans will invade before the rains make the ground too soft for their tanks. My superiors will want our force disposed to halt them as soon as is practicable. But we are too few. We need more men.'

'We need trained and armed men, not an unarmed rabble,' Willan said firmly. 'That settles it. We'll change location as soon as we are able. Morgan, Fraser, your job is to hunt up as much in the way of provisions as you can. Kigoma and Okello, give them details for foraging parties. Geary, I want those recruits who joined us recently to be discharged – but *after* they've helped with the loading of the equipment. I reckon it'll take about three trips to get everything into position.'

Another rattle of thunder and flash of lightning from outside. They paused a second, and soon they could hear something else: the sound of rain hitting the roof above them.

Fraser leaned out of a window and whistled softly. Cool air was coming in the open end of the hut, along with a fine water vapour.

'It's fucking tipping it down,' the Scot said. 'Rain like you wouldn't believe.'

'Great,' Willan said with heavy sarcasm. 'It'll make digging trenches even more fun. Still, it'll ground their aircraft, with any luck. Prentiss, any ideas on why they attacked, and how they found us?'

The rain was a thundering roar outside. Prentiss had to raise his voice to be heard.

'Stragglers from the steamer probably gave away the camp's location. I have a feeling the choppers were doing a reconnaissance. Maybe they got trigger-happy, or maybe they had orders to level the camp; my bet is the former. If they really wanted this place taken out, they'd have used MiGs. We just got unlucky, that's all.'

'Unlucky,' Willan repeated, angry. 'That's one way of putting it, I guess. Tell me, Prentiss – and Kigoma – when we finally take our positions in the Kagera salient, will we be completely on our own, or is there hope of reinforcement?'

Kigoma said nothing. It was Prentiss who spoke again.

'Your job is to buy time, Willan. At worst, you will blunt the Ugandan advance long enough for the militias that Nyerere is setting up to come into play. At best, you may even hold the enemy long enough for the rains to bog down his vehicles and give him second thoughts about the whole enterprise.'

'Just so we know,' Willan said. 'Okello, what about you? You'll be fighting against your countrymen.'

'I want to see Amin dead,' the Ugandan exile said simply. 'I want to see my country free of death squads. I will fight whoever tries to stop me.'

The rain poured down outside, a steady torrent. It sounded like a waterfall.

'Gentlemen, you have your orders,' Willan said at last. If there are no questions, then I suggest we get to work. There's a lot to do.'

The meeting broke up, the assembled men exiting the half-ruined hut to battle their way through the downpour outside. In minutes the camp was heaving with hundreds of armed men who worked steadily and relentlessly to load up the trucks with what had been salvaged from the ruin of their camp.

Less than three hours later the first long convoy began splashing and grinding its way along the muddy track to the north, to where they were to make their stand. Silent people watched them from the roadside as the heavy trucks and half-tracks rolled along, and all the while the rain fell without let-up, turning the roads into deepening quagmires and shrouding the horizon. Miles ahead, in the thick of the rain shadow, the Kagera foamed brown and white between its banks, and beyond that the Ugandan–Tanzanian border lay quiet and empty under the rain.

*　　*　　*

Lieutenant-Colonel Kasese stared out at the rain. Across the parade ground the T-55 tanks of his regiment were parked in rows, looking like great prehistoric beasts squatting asleep, the mud thickening around their tracks.

He turned and looked at Flight Lieutenant Ngoro again.

'You're quite sure it was a training camp?'

'Yes, sir. On our first pass they had several hundred men lined up for parade – no uniforms or weapons, just civilian men. But there were uniformed NCOs and officers. It looked like an intake of recruits. We also saw an assault course.'

'How much damage did you do?'

'We killed scores of them. And when we left the entire place was on fire. Must have been our tracers.'

'You said that Oyite's helicopter was destroyed by a missile.'

'Yes, sir, or a rocket. Probably shoulder-launched. After that, we decided it would be prudent to leave.'

Kasese nodded silently. Both good and bad. He would be able to confirm to his superiors that the Tanzanians were training large numbers of men, and that one training camp had almost certainly been destroyed. But he would also have to admit that Ugandan Army helicopters had openly and without provocation launched an attack on Tanzanian soil, inflicted high casualties and suffered some in return. He could not quite decide if the good and the bad cancelled each other out, and so was decidedly cool with Ngoro. The orders he had given the pilot had been ambiguous enough – just – for him to wash his hands of the affair if need be and declare that the man had exceeded his authority. That was why Ngoro was sweating and uneasy.

'I take it you cannot fly in this weather.'

'No, sir. All aircraft are grounded while the rain lasts.'

Kasese swore – a rare thing for him. He could not send an aircraft out to verify the camp's destruction then. Best to play it safe.

He was about to lean forward and tell Ngoro in no uncertain terms that the pilot had exceeded his authority, thereby earning himself a probable death sentence, when there was a knock at the door.

'Yes!' he barked, angry at being interrupted.

The orderly came in bearing a note.

'Your pardon, sir, but this just came by dispatch rider from Kampala.'

'Dispatch rider!' Kasese snorted. The rains must have brought down the lines.

He opened the note. It contained a terse set of instructions, and at the bottom, the signature of Amin himself. Kasese read through it once, twice, then sat down. Within seconds he stood up again. He was smiling. Ngoro breathed a little easier.

Kasese looked up from the note at last, still smiling.

'You may go, Flight Lieutenant. I attach no blame to you for your little skirmish; in fact you did well. Kindly ask my adjutant to step in on your way out.'

Vastly relieved, Ngoro stood up, saluted, then exited swiftly. A few minutes later Captain Bukima stepped in.

'Colonel?'

'Sit down, Bukima. We have orders from Kampala, from Amin himself. The invasion is on.'

Bukima leaned forward in his chair. 'When?'

'We must be ready to move in two days. The Simba Regiment will be the vanguard for the entire army.'

Bukima looked suddenly thoughtful.

'Two days – that should be enough to get everything organized. But if the rains keep up, the Kyaka road will be a swamp in two days. We could have problems with the tanks.'

'I know. Our advance must be swift and irresistible. The weather will probably be our greatest foe; there are no Tanzanian formations worth mentioning between here and Dodoma.'

'A pity the rains are early.'

'Indeed. From now until the new year the roads will only get worse – you know what they are like after several weeks of rain. Even the hard-surfaced highways will be swept with floods, mudslides and fallen trees. So we must move as rapidly as possible.'

'What about air support?' Bukima asked. 'Can MiGs fly in this?'

'No. If the rains ease a little, then we can expect some close-combat support, but not until then.'

'Our objective?'

'Initially, at least, the Kagera.'

'So. We have almost twenty miles to penetrate. How long do we have?'

Kasese looked at the note he still held in one hand.

'He is following the scenario we planned earlier in the summer, but is giving us more time due to the weather. Two days at most to the Kagera. Within four we must be dug in in force along the river.'

'That should not be a problem,' Bukima said, 'if resistance is light.'

'It will be.'

'What about these mercenary camps we have been hearing about, Colonel?'

'The one whose existence we confirmed was destroyed by Ngoro's helicopters.'

'Excellent. Then we will face nothing but a few hastily assembled militias.'

'Indeed. It promises to be a glorious campaign, Bukima.'

The two men looked at one another. They both knew that the only reason Idi Amin was sending his army into Tanzania was to head off troubles closer to home. The regime was shaky; there had been news of a regiment mutinying up north only last week. But still, they were both soldiers. The prospect of an easy war was rather pleasing; it was their *raison d'être*, after all.

'Will you want the officers assembled for a preliminary briefing?' Bukima asked.

'Yes. This evening. And have a Warning Order made up. Two days' notice to move. I want all the vehicles prepped and the necessary stores issued.'

'What about a reconnaissance, Colonel? Do you want me to send out a company in advance of the main body?' Bukima was following classic Soviet military doctrine.

'No, not this time. A small troop perhaps, but no more. Surprise must be total. Ngoro's mission confirmed that there is virtually nothing to oppose us for two hundred miles south of the border. I trust his information.'

'Very well, Colonel. If you'll excuse me, I'll start making the necessary arrangements.'

Bukima stood up and saluted, then left with a spring in his step.

Kasese rose and went to the window again. The rain seemed unending, like a precursor to some biblical flood. But it came every year; it was just early this time. A pity. It would not affect the end result of the campaign, though. Soon his tanks would be rolling across the border into Tanzania.

10

'Bastard,' Mick Morgan hissed. 'Bastard, bastard, bastard.'

He kicked the firmly embedded wheel of the M35 Studebaker truck one last time, then wiped his face with his bush hat and raised his voice to a commanding shout.

'All right, lads: spades and planks. Let's get to it.'

The convoy was halted along a swamp-like stretch of unsurfaced road. The heavy trucks had carved deep ruts in the slippery mud, and now yet another of them had bogged down. It happened with infuriating frequency, and the men had become practised at freeing the big vehicles from the clutch of the mud. They jumped down now with planks, sheets of corrugated iron and spades, and went to work. Ordinarily, they would have attached a cable to the vehicle in front and towed the stuck Studebaker free, but they had found more and more that this tactic resulted in two vehicles being bogged down instead of one. So instead they resorted to the filthy, laborious, time-consuming work of freeing the embedded wheels by hand.

This was the third convoy that had left the Mwanza camp, and, everyone hoped, the last. Already, three companies of SBS-trained men were digging in to the north, carving trenches for themselves out of the rain-soaked ground and clearing fields of fire. The last two companies – three hundred men under Morgan and Kigoma – were perched on the backs and in the beds of the trucks and half-tracks that lined this quagmire of a road, still eighty miles from their objective. They were averaging about five miles per hour, a pace which infuriated Morgan.

Kigoma came splashing down the track towards the SBS soldier. They were all covered with mud, wet through and seething with insect bites and ticks, but they noticed these things no more than they noticed the constant rain. They were a fact of life.

'The two lead vehicles are stuck also,' Kigoma said wearily. 'And there's been a mudslide about a mile ahead, the villagers tell me. We will have to clear it, or take an alternative route.'

'Is there one?' Morgan snapped. His eyes were red-rimmed with tiredness; he hadn't slept in almost three days.

'I don't know. I will take some men and find out. But we won't be able to rendezvous with the rest of the battalion today; it's too late.'

'All right, Kigoma, do that. See if there's a suitable track which gets us out of all this shit.'

The Tanzanian officer splashed away through the mud.

Morgan left his men straining and digging at the wheels of the embedded Studebaker and hauled his radio out of the cab. It was a PRC 353. Predictably, he could not contact Willan. It was still too far, and the rain was interfering with the transmissions.

'Like being back in the fucking Stone Age,' he groused to himself. Willan had hoped to have the battalion assembled and dug in by the next day at the latest, but that had all gone west now. At least the Ugandans would be having the same problems; that was one consolation. Morgan replaced the radio, then bent and began digging with the rest of the men at the immobilized wheels of the truck. Better late than never, he hoped.

Willan surveyed the company positions one by one. They were beginning to take shape. The men had been digging and sandbagging for two solid days and they were filthy, exhausted and hungry.

The battalion, as he called it now, was in position about eight miles north of Kyaka, less than twelve miles from the Ugandan border. It was placed astride the only decent road which led south into Tanzania, and was situated on a gentle rise which gave the companies good fields of fire. Willan had considered placing the position on the reverse slope of the rise but then decided against it. His troops were too green to allow enemy tanks to engage them at close range. Better to see the enemy coming from afar, or from as far as was possible in the rainy mist.

Six miles back, north of Kyaka, the Kagera rolled along, swollen between its banks. There was a concrete bridge spanning its flow just north of the village. Willan prayed that it would not be washed away. It represented his men's only escape route. It was bad tactics to allow his formation to be backed up against a river, but Kigoma and Okello had assured him that the bridge was a strong one and had never been washed away by even the most savage of rains. In addition, Prentiss had insisted that the battalion make a stand north of the river, otherwise the entire salient would be surrendered to the enemy without a fight, and he would be given a huge political advantage.

Politics again. It had dictated Willan's stategy, but his tactics were his own. He had placed his three existing companies in the classic two up, one back posture. Okello's company was to the left of the road; Kigoma's – under the temporary command of Geary – was to the right. Behind them both was a company of the greener troops under Fraser, giving depth and support to the forward companies. Because of the rising ground, they could bring their weapons to bear over the heads of the forward positions.

Out on the flanks, Willan had sited a series of trenches for the RPG1s, facing in at right angles to the road so as to catch the advancing armour in their vulnerable flanks. The entire position was slightly concave. Okello had told him with a grin that it resembled the old Zulu 'buffalo' formation, of two horns and a chest.

Between and slightly to the rear of the two forward companies were sited a pair of GPMGs mounted on tripods for sustained fire. If need be, these weapons could fire accurately in the dark, since they could be directed by bearing and elevation, and Willan had already mapped out a series of likely targets for them. The only problem was that there was not a lot of ammo for them – for anyone, come to that. That was something they'd just have to live with, like the rain and the leeches and the mosquitoes.

Out to the front of the forward companies, the SBS men had sited a minefield. They had only a few of the heavy anti-tank mines, so most of the field was composed of anti-personnel mines, or 'Elsies'. Hopefully, after the first few tanks had been wasted, the infantry would debus and advance straight into the minefield.

There was very little else in the way of field defences. Coils of wire were strung out forward of the position, but these were rudimentary two-coil affairs. They simply did not have the resources for more.

The riflemen of the companies were in four-man fire trenches, all sited so that their arcs of fire interlocked and were thus mutually supporting. There was good depth to the position, but Willan worried about his flanks. He could cater for a head-on attack only. If the Ugandans started getting smart and tried to roll up his flanks he would be in trouble.

Which was why he kept scanning the road to the south with his binoculars. He needed the other two companies that were still in transit from the Mwanza camp under Morgan and Kigoma. When they arrived he would site them off to each flank, to catch out any Ugandan attempt to sidestep the position. But there was no sign of them, and the day was getting along. They were probably bogged down somewhere.

The men had had nothing to eat today, as foraging parties could not be spared and, in any case, the countryside around here was pretty much deserted. They were on their last legs, Willan thought, watching them as they shovelled the mud out of their trenches and filled thousands of sandbags. No overhead protection was available, as he didn't have the necessary stores. But no planes could fly in this weather anyway – a small crumb of comfort.

The entire position housed some four hundred men. It was six hundred yards wide and half that in depth. And it was the only organized resistance the nation of Tanzania could offer at the moment to any invasion from Uganda. Willan had to chuckle at the madness of it. Here he was, a sergeant in the SBS, an ex-Marine, effectively commanding a battalion, the job of a colonel. And not a sea, river or lake in sight. Plenty of water, though. All the trenches had a foot of rainwater in them, and the men had to keep bailing them out. Very soon there would be the first cases of trench foot, and God knows what else in this climate. If the Ugandans didn't attack within a week or two, he had a feeling he would have to abandon the position anyway for the health of his men. Now there was a paradox.

Some of the clearing parties were filtering back into the position in single file, Gordon and Hill leading them through the mines. They had cleared an adequate field of fire to the front, but had left the thick brush to the flanks to conceal the RPG positions and hinder the approach of vehicles. It would provide cover for any attacking infantry, but that could not be helped.

Willan went over things in his mind for the fiftieth time. Had he forgotten anything?

Was there anything else to be done? He had half-rations for three days, but if the Ugandans had not invaded by then he would have to send out foraging parties once more; he couldn't keep everybody stood-to for ever. And Prentiss was in Dodoma, trying to get supplies and ammunition forwarded to him. He could think of nothing else to do. Except wait.

From Mbarara the road turned east, snaking though a series of bare hills before turning south. It was a dry-season road, which meant that it was near impassable during the rainy season, being totally unsurfaced. But the rains had been falling for only three days, and it had not yet metamorphosed into the river of mud that it would become.

A trio of French-built Savarin armoured cars rolled along to either side of the road, their big wheels churning ditches in the waterlogged earth. Their commanders had head and shoulders out of the small turrets and were cursing their drivers for the way the vehicles slewed and skidded. They were the advance element of the Simba Mechanized Regiment, a token reconnaissance of the ground ahead, and they had been on the move for almost a day and a half. Their crews were already fed up with

the unending struggle to keep the vehicles
moving, and the car interiors were dripping
with water and dank with sweat. Finally the
commander radioed back to the main body
that the road ahead was clear. There was
little to see through the curtain of the rain
anyway, and the afternoon was wearing on.
The Tanzanians had nothing to match the
force that was slogging up the road behind
him. His crews stopped the cars and took their
ease, struggling to light sodden cigarettes and
exchanging banter about what they would do
to the Tanzanians if they finally caught up with
them. The women in particular.

A few miles behind them, the main body of
the regiment was powering forward through
the muck. The T-55s had the broad tracks of
all Soviet tanks, and were making a respectable
pace, their 100mm guns traversing to left and
right to cover the hillsides to either side of
the road.

The T-55 was an early generation of Soviet
tank, without night-fighting capabilities and
mounting only one 7.62mm machine-gun for
anti-infantry work. It also was not universally
fitted with radios. Only the troop commanders
were in radio contact with each other and with
the commanding officer of the regiment. The

other crews had to look to their officers' vehicles to see where to go and what to do. But many of the tank crews felt that the mere presence of the metal monsters would be enough to overawe any enemy they might encounter, and they were both happy and confident as they roared south through the mud and rain.

Behind them the BRDMs and BMPs that housed the infantry lurched and whined their way through the huge ruts the tanks had carved. Many of the men were half asleep, lulled by the boredom of the journey. Others talked quietly among themselves. A very few cleaned their weapons and checked their equipment. Their officers had told them they were to expect little resistance. They had crossed the Tanzanian border without a shot being fired, and the sense of anticipation had left most of them. Now they were merely bored, their limbs aching from the primitive seating in their vehicles.

In a tank towards the middle of the long, straggling column, Colonel Kasese squinted over his map and cursed the water that was trickling down his neck. Blasted rain. But they were making good time. At this rate the lead elements of the regiment might make it to the Kagera before sunset, and he would have a presence on the objective more than twenty-four hours ahead of schedule. Nothing could stop him now.

'What was that?' Geary asked Willan, frowning and cocking his head to one side.

'I can't hear anything,' the SBS sergeant replied, listening. It was hard to hear anything above the hissing of the rain and the chatter of some of the men who were putting the finishing touches to their trenches. Most of the soldiers in the battalion were sitting on the lips of the trenches. They didn't want to stand in the water-filled holes any longer than they had to.

'There it is again. What do you make of it, Sarge?' Geary asked.

Again, Willan listened. This time he thought he heard something. A faint rattle-rumble in the distance. He and Geary looked at each other.

'Christ,' Geary said softly. 'Tanks.'

'Call stand-to,' Willan said at once. 'Get everyone into their trenches. It looks like they're on their way.'

'Right, Sarge.' The corporal hurried off to the company he was commanding in lieu of the absent Kigoma. Willan cursed fluently. There would be no time for the two companies delayed on the road to join him now. He would have to make do with what he had, which wasn't much. What he would have given for a battery of 105mms! Still, beggars would ride if wishes were horses.

'Stand to!' the cry went back and forth across the position. NCOs were kicking into the trenches those who were reluctant or slow to obey the order. Within minutes the slope on which the battalion was dug in seemed almost empty except for the dots of heads above sandbags and the bristling muzzles of weapons.

Willan threw himself into his own trench alongside his radio operator, a bright young Ugandan named Myebe, and two other men designated as runners. This was Battalion HQ, such as it was, and was located behind the sustained-fire machine-guns which lay between and behind the two forward companies.

The noise was clearer now; a sound to strike fear in the heart of any infantryman. The tracks of tanks.

Willan took up the handset of the PRC 351.

'Bravo One and Two, this is Zero. Over.'

'Send. Over.'

'Enemy armour coming up the road to your front. Open up on my order only. Over.'

'Bravo One. Roger, out.'

'Bravo Two. Roger, out.'

The two Bravo call-signs were Hill and Gordon, each commanding a detachment of RPG7-armed men off to the flanks. Willan trusted them to open fire when the time was right.

'Alpha One, Two and Three, this is Zero. Over.'

'Send. Over.'

'Wait for Bravo call-signs to initiate contact before opening up. Over.'

'Roger, out.'

The Alphas were the three company commanders, Okello, Geary and Fraser to the rear. Willan hoped they would be able to control the barely trained men under them. Still, the NCOs he had were shaping up pretty well and should be able to keep a grip on things.

Everyone could hear it now: tank engines roaring and the shrill squeak and rattle of tracks. A murmur of whispers swept the position and then was still.

They rolled into sight in one long, dark line of vehicles coming down from the north. There were no flanking units that Willan could see as he swept the ground with his binos, and no lead reconnaissance elements. Simply a long line of tanks, and behind them, assorted armoured personnel carriers. Did they think they were out for a Sunday drive or what?

The trenches and foxholes of his waiting infantry would be almost impossible to spot through the murk and the limited viewports of the tanks. With any luck, he would be able to let them get to within point-blank range. The 100mm guns of T-55s were accurate out to a kilometre, which was not much for a main battle tank these days, but it still outranged his RPG7s. They had to get closer, much closer, or else they could stand off and bombard his positions while he was almost powerless to reply.

He held the handset of the radio against his ear with one hand while the other held the binos up to his eyes. Closer, closer . . .

'Come on, you fuckers,' he grated in a low voice. 'Just a little farther. Blind bastards.'

Now. He clamped the pressel switch in his handset with his fingers.

'All Bravo call-signs, open fire at will. I repeat, open fire at will.'

All hell broke loose.

*   *   *

In less than a second the three lead T-55s erupted into miniature infernos of flame and oily smoke. The turret of one was blown clean off and sent careering across the road.

At once the tanks to the rear of the destroyed vehicles broke off to left and right, bypassing their knocked-out comrades. But a second wave of RPG rounds cannoned into them, hitting their vulnerable side armour and obliterating them too. A huge fireball rose up as the reserve fuel tanks of one armoured vehicle exploded. A few insect-like crewmen tumbled out of hatches, their clothing on fire. The sound of exploding ordnance hid their screaming.

The next troop accelerated madly and swerved off the road, throwing up fountains of mud from their madly spinning tracks. The gunners began firing the main guns blindly up the slope to their front, and kept coming with their machine-guns barking little jets of flame into the overcast evening.

The road was like a burning scrapyard. Pools of petrol blazed as surviving crewmen fled back down the column. Other tanks were scattering off the road, which had become a death-trap, and were firing blind up the hillsides around them. Some of the infantry had debussed and were sprinting to the front, while others sat tight in their vehicles, no doubt wondering what the hell was going on. The sustained-fire machine-guns in the centre of Willan's battalion opened up, guided by Parker, who was down there adjusting their sights. The infantrymen ran into a wall of lead and were bowled over. They took cover behind the burning hulks of their armour and began firing back.

Tanks further down the column had shaken out into formation and were now advancing relentlessly, firing as they came. The slope below Willan began to erupt with shell bursts. Many of his men had opened up with their rifles, though they could do little damage with them. The enemy infantry were cowering behind wrecked tanks or sitting tight in their vehicles, still some five hundred yards away. But it would serve to distract the enemy from the real threat; the hidden anti-tank weapons on his flanks.

The T-55s were in attack formation now, ploughing through the soft earth and seemingly hell-bent on running straight over Willan's position. Then the RPGs boomed yet again, three on each flank. Willan saw two hits;

two tanks blew up and exploded. Another was hit in the track and ground to a halt, its crew bailing out only to be mown down by the SF machine-guns directed by Parker.

But the heavy tank rounds were having some effect now. They were erupting all over the slope to the front, though thankfully the heavy, wet earth absorbed some of the energy of the high-explosive rounds. Willan saw some of the forward foxholes collapsing, men scurrying from the wet holes only to be cut down by the heavy automatic fire that seemed to be tearing up the entire hillside. He thought he heard Geary's voice shouting orders but could not be sure. The foremost T-55s were almost on top of the leading foxholes. RPG rounds raised a storm of metal and muck around the lead enemy vehicles. Another two tanks destroyed. The entire plain forward of the position seemed to be ablaze with burning tanks, the smoke from the fires like a black fog that hung unmoving in the humid air. Willan wondered how much ammunition the anti-tank weapons had left. The pressure would soon become too much to bear.

Infantry now. They had debussed *en masse*

at last and were advancing behind the metal hulls of the tanks.

'Incoming!' someone – Parker perhaps – yelled in English, and Willan heard the distinctive plopping sound of mortar rounds. They must have set their vehicle-mounted mortars up somewhere in the rear. Quick work.

The world exploded, becoming a fountain of muck and earth. The enemy mortarmen walked the rounds up the hill right through the position. Willan wiped dirt from his eyes, spat out mud, and tried to see what was going on.

The SF machine-guns were silent – they had taken a direct hit. The hillside was beginning to resemble a vision of the Somme. Some of the men were running from their trenches in panic, only to be blown apart by a fresh barrage of mortar shells. The tanks were still advancing.

'Fuck,' Willan growled. He squeezed the handset, and said, 'Bravo call-signs, this is Zero. Send sitrep. Over.'

After a moment, he recognized Hill's voice crackling back through the earpiece. It was almost impossible to hear over the thunderous roar of the battle.

'Bravo One, we have tanks advancing to our

front, maybe one zero zero metres away. We are down to four rounds. Request permission to bug out. Over.'

'Fuck,' Willan said again, in a whisper this time. This was where being a CO really sucked.

'Roger, Bravo One. Permission denied. Hold your ground. I say again, hold your position at all costs. Over.'

'Roger, out.'

'Zero, this is Bravo Two. Overheard your last and will comply. Over,' Gordon's voice said, over on the right.

'Roger, out,' Willan told him. He felt like a murderer.

But he was positive that the momentum of the attack could not be kept up for long. The enemy formation had taken dreadful punishment, and couldn't know how close its foes were to breaking. If he could only get the battalion to hang on for a little longer, he was sure that he could outbluff the enemy commander. A few more minutes.

He knew that what he was doing was right, but it didn't make him feel any better.

Colonel Kasese was hoarse with shouting over the tank radio. He wanted to go forward, to find out what was happening, but that would be to invite his own destruction. Instead he was demanding situation reports from his officers at the head of the column, and getting nothing but garbled, panic-stricken shouting in return. All he knew was that the enemy were dug in ahead in unknown strength, with plenty of anti-tank weapons, and that they had already taken out almost a third of his tanks. He had called forward the 120mm vehicle-mounted mortars, but there was little else he could do except order his crews to advance and hope they would overrun whoever was making the stand up ahead.

Inconceivable! That an entire armoured regiment might be brought to a halt and roundly thrashed by a motley bunch of militias scraped up at the last minute. No, there was more to this than met the eye.

But that was for later. For now, he had to destroy the enemy, to drive him back into the river. He kicked his driver's shoulder and told him to move forward, his impatience and outrage finally getting the better of him. The tank roared towards the inferno of wrecks and explosions and vehicles that was the head of the column.

He could glimpse men running through the

flames and the smoke: his own infantry and the surviving tank crews pelting to safety. His tank shuddered with the impact as his driver shunted a wrecked vehicle out of his way, off the road.

Other tanks were retreating. The sighting system on the T-55 was so primitive that the vehicle had to slow to a crawl or halt altogether every time it fired. These tanks were falling back and firing while still at full speed. Kasese thumped his viewfinder in fury. Cowards!

Two troops raced past him in the wrong direction. Many of the tanks had the figures of men clinging to them. Others had sustained minor hits and were leaking clouds of black smoke. He saw one explode as he watched, the main gun blown fifty feet up in the air.

'Cease retreating!' he yelled over the radio. 'All troops will cease retreating at once and resume the advance on the enemy position!'

It was no use; nothing but static came back by way of reply.

The tank rocked with a near miss; the enemy was ranging in on him now – the only vehicle not in retreat.

Kasese kicked out at the back of his driver's head.

176

'Get us out of here!' he ordered in a voice strangled by shame and fury.

The driver complied gladly, shoving the tank into reverse and then yanking viciously round on the steering sticks so that one track locked and the other spun madly. The heavy vehicle turned 180 degrees almost on its own axis, then roared off at full speed. Kasese cranked the turret round to look back at the receding enemy position. It was pock-marked with craters and overhung with smoke. A battalion position, at least, with anti-tank weapons deployed on the flanks to make a killing-ground of the road his tanks had moved up. The carcasses of his vehicles littered the battlefield. Over a dozen, if not more.

Even as his tank lurched and bounced under him, carrying him out of range, he was making plans for the next attack. They would regroup, reorganize and try again. He would destroy these Tanzanians whatever the cost.

'They're pulling back,' Willan said, squinting through the failing light and the endless rain. 'I don't believe it.'

A wave of relief and elation washed over him. They had actually halted an armoured regiment in its tracks and then sent it into headlong retreat. He felt like cheering.

'Zero, this is Bravo One. Over.' It was Hill, out on the left with the RPG detachment.

'Send. Over.'

'Bravo One. Last enemy vehicle eliminated five zero metres from our location, no ammo left. Trousers all brown. Over.'

Willan chuckled. Hill had made it, thank God.

'Roger, Bravo One. Fucking good work. Out to you. All call-signs, reorg. I repeat, reorg, and hold your positions. Out.'

There was still some desultory fire from the enemy infantry, but launching another attack seemed to be the furthest thing from their minds. And besides, it was getting dark, and he was almost sure the Ugandan Army had bugger-all in the way of night-sights.

Willan spoke into his mud-slimed handset again. Now that the battle was over for the moment, he felt like an old man, and had begun to realize how filthy, uncomfortable and hungry he was.

'All Sunrays, this is Zero. Make tracks to my location ASAP. Out.'

It took only a few minutes for the 'Sunrays' or unit commanders to rendezvous in Willan's trench, though it meant displacing Myebe and the two runners. The men looked utterly spent in the light of the brief African twilight, the rain trickling down their filthy faces.

'All right, lads,' Willan said quietly. 'This has to be quick; I want sitreps.'

Geary began.

'Eleven dead, fourteen wounded. We're down to three mags per man. No RPG rounds left.'

'Parker and the SFs?' Willan asked.

'He's dead, Sarge. One of the SF trenches took a direct hit. We've maybe five hundred rounds left for the other one.'

There was a silence. Parker had been a good bloke. They had all known him a long time, and knew his wife too.

'All right,' Willan said at last. 'Okello?'

The Ugandan exile squinted at a notebook in the dim light, wiping rain off the pages.

'Nine dead, seven wounded. About two mags per man – nothing else.'

'Fraser?' Willan asked the Scot, who had commanded the reserve company.

'No casualties, Sarge, but about a dozen of the blokes legged it during the scrap. It was too much for them, I suppose. We've still got about five mags per man.'

Willan looked grim, but made no comment. 'Hill and Gordon?'

Hill spoke up first. 'Two dead, no wounded. We lost an RPG and we've fuck-all ammo left.'

Gordon had an almost identical story to tell. When he had finished, Willan shone a small red penlight down on to the notebook he had been keeping track in.

'So we're down to about three hundred and fifty effectives, we're critically low on ammo and rations and we have no anti-tank capability worth speaking of.'

'Apart from that everything's just hunky-dory,' Fraser said sardonically.

'Any idea of how badly we hurt the enemy? Willy?'

Geary smiled. 'I think it's fair to say we fucked up his entire day, Sarge. I reckon we took out thirteen tanks and most of their crews, plus a shitload of infantry and a few armoured personnel carriers. I'd say we gave him one hell of a bloody nose.'

'But will he be back for more? Okello, what do you think?'

Okello's dark face was almost invisible.

'The commander of that regiment will have to take this position or he will answer for it with his own head. Yes, they will attack again, though they will do it differently next time, I think.'

'You think he'll start feeling for our flanks.'

'Yes. It is what I would do.'

Willan nodded. 'That settles it then. We've beaten him once, but we can't do so again. The position has become untenable. We're pulling out of this location tonight, under cover of darkness. We'll try and take what equipment we can with us, and the wounded, of course.'

'It's over six miles to the Kagera,' Geary pointed out.

'I know. So this will have to go smoothly and quietly. Rear units first. Okello, Willy, I want you both to leave two sections apiece until the very end to counter any probes or recces the enemy feel like doing. Hill, take over the remaining SF. Jock, I want you and your men to set up a couple of miles down the road and let everyone else filter through. You'll be the rearguard once Okello and Willy's men finally bug out.'

'There's still a hell of a lot of Elsies buried to our front,' Jock Fraser pointed out. 'Their infantry never advanced far enough to set them off. It'll slow them down if they try any monkey business during the night.'

'I know. If he does try anything before dawn, it'll be with infantry. T-55s are fuck-all use in the dark. We'll move the wounded first, two men carrying each casualty. Gag them – we can't afford any unnecessary noise. Next will be the heavier equipment. Hill, you get the remaining SF to Jock's company and join him in the rearguard. The surviving RPGs will join you too.'

'Timings?' Geary asked.

'I'll figure them out and send them to you by runner. In the meantime, get your units prepared to move. Willy, Okello, keep a sharp lookout to your front in case they try something silly like a night assault. Any questions?'

'Yes, Sarge,' Geary said. 'What about Morgan and Kigoma and the other two companies?'

'We should meet them on the road if they're anywhere near getting here yet. There are three trucks still in Kyaka; we'll use those to take the wounded south to the hospital at Kemondo.'

'Where do we take up our next position?' Okello asked.

'On the southern bank of the Kagera. We

have to cross the Kagera bridge, and then we have to hold it.'

'For how long?' Hill asked.

'For as long as it takes.'

'I knew it,' Fraser said with a wry grin. 'We're in a John Wayne film. I had my suspicions before, but now I'm sure of it.'

'All right, lads, let's get to it,' said Willan. 'I'll forward the timings to you as soon as I can.'

The night passed quietly. A few tanks were still burning, making orange bonfires in the darkness, and from time to time one of the wounded could be heard moaning, but otherwise there was no sound but for the night insects and the occasional roar of a lion, off in the bush. Later in the evening a pack of hyenas prowled the battlefield like a bunch of ghouls, foraging among the corpses. However, a burst of fire from an alert sentry saw them off.

Around midnight it stopped raining and when the men looked up they could see the clouds clearing a little, stars peeping down out of a blue-black sky. By that time the withdrawal was well under way.

It did not go quite to plan. In the darkness it was easy for the men to lose their sense of direction, and those bearing the wounded made agonizingly slow progress. By the early hours the battalion position was empty but for the four holding sections of Okello and Geary, but the line of weary, burdened and wounded men trailed for half a mile to the south with their NCOs and the remaining SBS men constantly redirecting the lost and the exhausted. Some men sat down and slept, so weary were they, and the NCOs had to kick and shove them awake, make them move again. All organization was lost in the confusion of the lightless retreat, and platoons and companies merged into a single trudging crocodile of tired men.

Once they were over the brow of the hill, and in dead ground, the SBS men shone red pencil torches to show the way to go, and the long column tightened up somewhat. But they were losing people all the same. Soldiers who had had enough dropped out to snatch some precious sleep. Men too enervated to go any further abandoned their weapons and equipment to lighten their load and stumbled on unarmed. It was impossible to exert control silently, in darkness, over men who had simply given up.

Finally they were far enough away for

Fraser to deploy his company as rearguard. The last of Okello and Geary's men had left the position and they were a mere four miles from the bridge across the Kagera. But Fraser's company of green recruits seemed to have melted away into the night. He could muster barely sixty men when he stopped to redeploy around two a.m. There was nothing to do but to keep following the plan. He made his remaining soldiers dig shell-scrapes, though some of the younger men, still teenagers, were almost weeping with tiredness. Then he settled down to wait. Hill stayed with him, manning the last SF gun with a few volunteers. The rest of the battalion continued to trek south towards their objective.

The sun was coming up. Already the sky was light in the east. From his position on a low hill to the west of the road, Willan could see the Kagera glinting in the first rays of the dawn sunlight. A mile away perhaps. The Kyaka road was empty in the morning sun, the bridge over the river deserted.

He looked down into the shallow valley below him. Now that there was light to see, the NCOs were trying to gather together the scattered remnants of the battalion. The withdrawal, Willan thought bitterly, had cost him more men than the actual battle; but that was a fact of military life. Sometimes victory was as disruptive as defeat.

He tried to count numbers on the ground but gave up. There were a lot less than there should be at any rate. Holding the bridge would be no easy task if the enemy were as belligerent as they had proved themselves the day before.

He looked up at the clearing sky. It was a blessed relief, the absence of rain, but it had a dark side too. Now the Ugandan Air Force would be able to take to the air, and at the moment his men were sitting ducks.

He peered south again, to the muddy Kyaka road. Where the hell were Morgan and Kigoma, and the three hundred men who were with them? He needed them now, needed them badly.

Then he heard it. The crump of heavy guns to the north and the sudden rattle of automatic fire. Fraser's rearguard was under attack.

11

The Ugandan Army advanced as soon as the sun began to rise. Colonel Kasese rested his elbows on the turret hatch of his tank and studied the terrain before him through binoculars. It had taken most of the night to reorganize his forces, look after his wounded and put the finishing touches to his new plan.

While two troops of his tanks stood off less than a mile from the enemy front line and bombarded it with high-explosive shells, his infantry led this fresh attack, debussing from their armoured personel carriers a hundred yards short of the enemy position and then darting forward by fire teams and sections, crouching behind the hulks of tanks, taking advantage of every increment of cover.

At the same time most of his remaining tanks, supported by more infantry, had moved out on either side of the road and were feeling round the flanks of the enemy defences. This way the Tanzanians would be assaulted from three sides at once.

The explosions of the tank bombardment ripped the quiet of the early morning apart. Then the infantry moved forward and the bombardment crept up the hill, tearing the ground to shreds for the second time in two days. Kasese thought the enemy had been strangely quiet up until now. He scanned with his binos and saw his infantry hit the ground and fire up the hill. Several of his men were writhing on the ground and there were three smoking craters among them, then other small eruptions of dirt among their ranks as they moved forward. Mortars? No. Mines, of course.

He spoke into his hand mike.

'Songezi Company, hold your ground. Do not advance further – you are in a mine-field. Over.'

He received a brief acknowledgement. The infantry went to ground among the barbed wire of the first enemy positions. A few moments later T-55s were swarming all over the enemy trenches. They had turned the enemy flanks, crashing through the thick brush on either side of the road. But something was not quite right. Kasese studied the battlefield intently, suspicion growing into certainty.

He thumped his fist down on the steel roof of the turret. Of course – the position was empty! The Tanzanians must have withdrawn during the night!

He began giving fresh orders over the radio. They were brief and simple. He watched as the tanks on the hillside acted on them immediately, turning on to the road and heading south. He ordered his infantry to mount up and follow the armour. Then he leapt off the tank and ran through the deep mud towards the communications truck farther back in the column. He needed a long-range radio, one that would reach as far as Entebbe. Allah be praised for the clear weather!

Half an hour after Fraser's men had heard the sound of the heavy guns in the distance, they saw the lead elements of the Ugandans moving up the road towards them. Jock had precisely eight rounds of ammunition left for the RPGs and was hefting one of the slim anti-tank weapons himself. Every round must count. He knew from Willan that the rest of the battalion were almost at the river but had still not crossed. Every minute that he could delay the enemy advance, therefore, would be a minute gained for the rest of the battalion to use in getting to safety.

He had dispersed the other three RPG7s outside his infantry positions. Their firers were holed up in camouflaged scrapes to east and west of the road, forward of his own location. They would fire their rounds and then bug out for the river, hopefully stalling the enemy armour and perhaps forcing the Ugandans to bring their infantry forward to spare the tanks any further casualties. That was the plan anyway.

The enemy had learned from the débâcle of yesterday. They had fanned out in attack formation, the tanks leading the way and the armoured personnel carriers powering along behind them. How far away now? Twelve hundred yards maybe. Almost within range of the forward-posted RPGs.

Three sudden flashes of light on the hillsides above the Ugandan armour. Fraser thought he could almost see the streak of one missile as it roared towards its target. Yes! Two enemy tanks had 'brewed up'. One was a complete wreck, a fireball. The other had been hit in the running gear and was disabled. Not bad.

The Ugandans started doing their headless

chicken routine again. If they'd had any sense they'd have cleared the route with infantry and kept the tanks in a supporting role, but Fraser wasn't complaining.

Another tank exploded. They were firing back now, and the infantry were debussing. Good. Fraser turned and waved at Hill in his SF shell-scrape. The other SBS man nodded. A second later a stream of tracer went arcing down the road from the tripod-mounted GPMG, picking off the enemy infantry, bouncing off the sides of tanks, generally playing merry hell.

Fraser saw one RPG team bug out from its hiding-place. They didn't get far before enemy fire cut them to shreds. There was no sign of the other two teams, but they had all done their job well. The enemy advance was disrupted, the Ugandans thrown off guard again.

Shit! Tank rounds were slamming into the ground all around him, hurling up huge geysers of dirt and stones and water. They must have spotted the infantry scrapes. The tanks were hanging back now, using their main armaments as support weapons for the advancing Ugandan infantry. That was showing a little more sense, Fraser thought, though he could have happily done without it.

He sighted down the RPG after checking that there was nobody to be caught in the back-blast, then fired the weapon at an advancing BRDM.

Bingo. The vehicle took the round squarely on the nose, and blew up. Fucking brilliant.

'Jock! Jock!' It was Hill.

'What is it?'

'The SF's out of ammo.'

Fraser looked at the advancing infantry to his front. His company, or what remained of it, were firing down the road for all they were worth, but they lacked the ammunition for a prolonged battle. They had done enough.

'Bug out!' he shouted at the top of his lungs, dropping the RPG and picking up his AK47 instead.

He waved his men out of their shallow scrapes while the tank rounds walked up and down the position and the enemy infantry fire ripped up the sodden ground. Soldiers falling everywhere, a huge chaos of bright flame and muck and screaming men.

'*Come on!*' He waved them back, and they tumbled out of the scrapes and began running. These troops were green; he tried to get them to stop and use fire and manoeuvre but it was no use. Panic had infected them now that they were on the retreat, and all Fraser's plans for an orderly, fighting withdrawal went for nothing. He cursed rabidly. Then a shell landed barely thirty feet from him and spun him through the air. He felt nothing but a lung-emptying impact along his left side and when he opened his eyes again the sky was blue and empty above him and the sounds of battle seemed far away, distant as a television in the next room.

He raised himself up on one elbow. His rifle had disappeared. The enemy infantry were barely fifty yards away, screaming like fiends and blazing away ammunition like it was going out of fashion. There was a pain in his gut. He looked down to see the coils of dirt-flecked and perforated intestine protruding from his ripped uniform, like a pile of greasy blue ropes.

'Aw, shit,' he groaned.

He drew his Browning to fire at the advancing enemy, but a burst of automatic fire thudded into him and threw him back again. He watched the blue sky once more, wondering what had happened.

Then the world went dark.

Willan heard the battle from where he stood in the middle of the Kagera bridge. The last stragglers were just crossing; he had two hundred men digging in on the southern bank, all that was left of the battalion. Gordon, Breckenridge and Geary, together with Okello and some of the better NCOs, were bullying the men into digging fresh trenches, getting together a detail to bring up the trucks from Kyaka.

The soldiers were like zombies or sleepwalkers. Most of them had had little or no rest for three days and nights. They were filthy and vermin-infested, bloodstained and ravenously hungry. Willan knew they were dangerously close to a transformation from military unit into mob. But there was little he could do about it. They had to fortify this position, hold it as long as they could. This time there would be no withdrawal. After the Kagera there was no defensive line for forty miles, and if the bridge fell, then the road would be open to Bukoba, one of Tanzania's main ports on Lake Victoria. The war would be lost, and Amin would be more securely in power than ever.

So they must hold. But how? They had perhaps ninety rounds of ammunition per man and morale was low. They had no heavy weapons, no anti-tank capability and no logistical support. It was as if, Willan thought bitterly, they had been entirely forgotten by the outside world and were fighting alone and forgotten against the full might of the Ugandans.

He looked north again. It sounded like a bombardment up there. Jock must be making one hell of a fight of it. He hoped the little bastard came out of it OK. Hill too. It was a shock losing Tony Parker like that. They couldn't even recover the body for his family.

No use in thinking like that. There were too many things to do here. Willan had already ordered the detail sent to collect the trucks to commandeer every gallon of petrol in Kyaka. He would do as the Hungarians had done, and fight Soviet tanks with petrol bombs if he had to.

He turned and looked south along the muddy road to Kyaka and beyond. If he faced facts, they had no hope of holding here longer than a few hours. But the last ace up his sleeve might yet appear. If Morgan and Kigoma could only get their fingers out and make an appearance. They would have the reserve ammunition, rations and the heavy Brownings of the M3s, as well as three hundred fresh men to call upon – if only those fucking trucks would just appear above the horizon.

He shook his head, then paused and listened again. The sounds of fighting to the north seemed to have sputtered out. The heavy guns had ceased booming and now there were only sporadic bursts of small-arms fire.

Geary joined him on the bridge, looking gaunt and filthy as a scarecrow in winter, his eyes sunk in his head.

'Sounds as though Jock's done a runner,' he said.

'I hope so,' Willan answered him.

'Well,' Geary said, 'he's a tricky bastard. They'll have their work cut out trying to nab him.'

'Too right,' Willan said. He knew that neither of them really believed what they were saying, but they had to say it.

'I guess they'll be on their way again soon,' Geary went on.

'Yeah. They'll be right in our laps in an hour or so. Let's get to work, Willy, and see if we can't give them another nasty surprise.'

They walked back to where the battalion was digging trenches for its next stand.

'What the fuck?' Morgan demanded.

The heavy military truck in which he was travelling swerved wildly to avoid the white civilian car which had come tearing out of a side-road in front of it. The car's horn was blaring madly and someone was waving out of the driver's window. Waving him down, Morgan realized.

'He wants us to stop,' Kigoma said, puzzled.

The car slowed and then came to a halt. The Studebaker had no choice but to halt behind it. Behind the first truck, two dozen other vehicles laden with equipment and covered with armed soldiers squelched to a halt in the deep, water-filled ruts of the dirt road. Men jumped off the trucks to see what the trouble was. Morgan sprang out of the cab of the lead vehicle with an AK47 in his fist. He was seething with anger.

William Prentiss emerged from the civilian car, still waving.

'What the fuck do you want?' Morgan yelled at him. 'Don't you know we're in a fucking hurry? We're behind time and every second counts. Get that bastard car of yours out of the way or, so help me, I'll fucking drive over it.'

The frustration of the past couple of days seemed to boil over in him. He knew that the battalion could be fighting for its life up in the north, and he was here manhandling ageing lorries through a sea of mud. And now this fucking spook wanted to stop for a chat. It was too much.

'Calm down,' Prentiss said sharply. 'I haven't stopped you for nothing. I have news you should know about.'

'Spill it then.'

There was someone else in the car. Morgan caught a glimpse of a blonde head. But that was not important now.

'The war has begun,' Prentiss said simply.

'What? When?'

'Amin's tanks crossed the border yesterday morning. They should have run into your lot by yesterday evening, if they made good time.'

'How do you know this?'

'My sources in Kampala, and the hurried telephone call of a man living in the village of Mutukula, near the border. He rang police headquarters in Bukoba, who relayed it to Mwanza and so on.'

'You're sure about this, Prentiss?'

'Perfectly.'

'Jesus Christ.' Morgan rubbed his chin with one large hand.

'Do you have any idea how the fighting has gone?'

'Some of the locals have been phoning any-one they can in the Tanzanian government or in any public services. The hospital at Bukoba has even been getting calls.'

'And?'

'Heavy fighting north of the Kagera. That's all I know.'

'Fuck,' Morgan said viciously. 'Jesus fucking Christ. Is the government doing anything about it, or are our men fighting alone up there?'

'The militias are being mobilized, but it's a slow business. I've been in touch with the Defence Ministry. They won't be able to get any reinforcements up to the Kagera before tomorrow at the earliest.'

'So we're the only reinforcements Willan can count on,' Morgan said, looking back along the line of vehicles and the men who were watching them intently from the truck beds.

'In a word, yes,' Prentiss said. 'I've been trying to get more ammunition and equipment forwarded to you from Dodoma, but it's a slow business. I wouldn't count on it for a while. What do you have in the convoy?'

'Three hundred men, the reserve ammu-nition, some RPG7s and a couple of Carl Gustav 84mms. Not a hell of a lot, but I'd best get it moving quickly. So thanks for the news, Prentiss, and now move that fucking car.'

'No. Let me lead the way. I know a pretty good road that leads to the west of Bukoba. I'll get you to Kyaka in a couple of hours.'

Morgan stared at him closely. 'You're on. Let's get moving.'

The Intelligence agent got back into his car while Morgan clambered back aboard the lead truck in the convoy. Morgan pumped his fist in the air and the engines of the heavy vehicles all began to thunder into life. A few moments later they were on their way again, headed north towards the Kagera.

The survivors of Fraser's company straggled across the bridge two hours after Willan had settled in the last of his own men. They were shattered, wild-eyed, many of them without weapons, others helping along wounded comrades. As the motley band hurried across the bridge, a filthy, bloody figure detached himself from them and stopped before Willan.

'Hi, Sarge. I've brought back as many as I could.'

It was Hill, though he was hardly recognizable. He swayed as he spoke and the rings under his eyes made him look like an old man.

'Where's Fraser?' Willan asked him.

'Dead. We took out another four or five tanks, maybe a platoon of infantry. But the withdrawal was fucked. You can't blame the men – they're only youngsters, and barely trained. We left behind the SF and all but one of the RPGs. Sorry, Sarge.'

Willan gripped him by the shoulder.

'You're sure Jock is dead?'

'Yes. A tank round got him. Shrapnel in the stomach. But we made them pay for it, the stupid bastards. They may have all the heavy stuff they want, but they're a bunch of amateurs. Last I saw they were still reorging on the position, running about like old women. It won't be long before they get their act together, though. It'll be infantry they hit us with, I think – that lead regiment has fuck-all tanks left.'

'You did good, Keith,' Willan said. 'Get behind the position and grab some kip, and if your lot have any ammo left, send it forward to the lads in the forward positions. We got water and some food out of Kyaka; it's over by the trucks. Make sure you all get a bite to eat.'

Hill smiled tiredly. 'It's going to be a long day.'

'Yes, it is.'

Hill staggered off.

Geary approached Willan.

'Jock's gone then?'

'Yes. Shrapnel, according to Hill.'

'Fuck. I always thought that little Scottish bastard was indestructible.'

'Me too. How are the Molotovs coming along?'

'We've got dozens of the things, and I've set up a few Elsies next to dug-in bottles of petrol on the approaches to the bridge.'

'You always were an evil little shit, Willy.'

'Yeah, well, it'll scare the living hell out of their infantry, and it might fuck up an APC or two. Armoured vehicles and burning petrol have never mixed too well . . . Sarge, how long do we have to hold them here? I don't want to piss on anyone's parade, but the men are on their last legs. We're down to less than two hundred effectives, we have maybe sixty wounded back in Kyaka, we're low on ammo and we're resorting to petrol bombs against T-55s. This isn't Budapest, you know, or Prague for that matter.'

'Okello tells me that the outfit we've been fighting is the Simba Regiment – the best they have. It's the premier armoured formation in the country, and we've been knocking seven shades of shit out of it for two days . . .'

'And getting it knocked out of us in return,' Geary put in.

'Yes, but they don't necessarily know that. They must be tearing their hair out in clumps right now. They expected to roll over a few militia and instead they've been fighting every step of the way, and losing tanks left right and centre. I agree with Hill – they'll use infantry against us next to save what armour they have left. That evens the score a little.'

'What about the Tanzanian government – do they even know what's going on?'

'I've sent men to Kyaka to get the word out any way they can. But we can't expect too much, not yet. We're going to be on our own for a while yet, Willy.'

'So where the fuck is that big cunt Morgan?'

'God knows. Probably stuck in a ditch somewhere. He'll be here, though, if he has to haul those trucks here by hand.'

But Geary did not seem to be listening. He held up a hand. 'Sarge, wait a minute. Can you hear that?'

'What is it, tanks again?'

'No. It's . . .'

Suddenly the noise became audible to Willan too. He swore, and went running for the shallow trenches the men were digging south of the bridge.

'Take cover!'

A flight of three MiG 15s, their swept-back wings unmistakable, burst into view over the hills to the north. The sky was filled with the roar of their engines.

'Incoming!' Geary yelled, then threw himself into the nearest shell-scrape.

They were using 200lb bombs, and swooped low into a hail of small-arms fire to deliver them. The first landed in the river, raising up a mountain of foam. Two more landed to the south of the battalion position, carving huge craters out of the wet earth. And two landed on target.

The aircraft wheeled and screeched off to the north, their mission over. The storm of small-arms fire which had greeted them seemed to have done no damage.

The centre of Willan's defences was a smoking ruin. Men were screaming and the cordite smell of the explosions choked their lungs.

At almost the same moment the first elements of the enemy armour appeared on the slopes of the hills to the north, the tanks standing back and laying down fire while the APCs roared on to their front.

Willan raised his head. He was half buried by soil, still deaf from the thunderous impact of the airstrike. He hauled himself out from under the debris, spitting dirt.

'Come on. Stand to! Here they come!'

Dazed men were raising their heads all around them, amazed at still being alive. The two bombs had taken out a full platoon; at least two dozen men had been vaporized by their impact and a dozen more were still screaming in agony, some of them waving the red stumps of amputated limbs.

'Jesus,' Willan said. 'Hill! Get your men forward! Start a casevac. The rest of you, look to your front!'

His radio was gone, obliterated by the strike. He could see other, higher-altitude jet trails in the sky heading out to the east. It seemed a full squadron of Ugandan planes was heading off on missions in Tanzania. Even over the crump of the tank rounds and the rattle of nearby small arms, Willan could hear the low thunder of bombing over the hills towards Lake Victoria. They must be bombing Bukoba. This was it then. This was their big push.

'Terrific,' he croaked.

While the battalion collected itself and the wounded were ferried to the rear, the Ugandan vehicles rolled at full speed down the hillsides towards the river. Swarms of BMPs and BRDMs, their vehicle guns flickering as they put down fire. There was nothing the defenders could do to halt them until they closed range.

The APCs halted at last, and the enemy infantry debussed scant yards in front of the river. An RPG flashed and one of the enemy vehicles exploded into fragments. Rounds began to tear up the ground all along the southern bank of the Kagera, and splashed white water from the river itself.

The Ugandan infantry ran into the first of the buried petrol-enhanced mines. Globes of fire erupted from the ground and engulfed whole sections of them as they advanced. Blazing figures threw themselves into the river or writhed on the muddy ground shrieking until the fire from Willan's men silenced them. For a few minutes it seemed that the air hanging over the position was full of nothing but noise and bullets and the roar of explosions as the tank rounds zoomed in. Some men took shelter in the deep craters left by the airstrike, forsaking the shallow scrapes they had dug for themselves. There was no time for orders; it was a grim, relentless fire-fight that seemed to go on for ever, the opposing forces battling it out within two hundred yards of each other like two boxers locked in a clinch.

But Willan's men were low on ammunition. Already some of them were cowering in their scrapes, keeping their heads down, their eyes shut tight. Others were scavenging for spare magazines from the bodies of the dead.

The Ugandans were rushing the bridge in fire teams and squads, but there was no cover there. Okello and a determined group of other Ugandan exiles were laying down a fierce fire that swept the enemy off the bridge and sent them reeling back, looking frantically for cover on the northern bank. But the enemy were moving up more APCs now, with infantry advancing at a crouch behind them.

Petrol bombs exploded in orange glory across the bridge as Geary led a handful of men to engage the advancing vehicles at point-blank range. Two of them went up in flames, their crews abandoning them only to be cut down by the fire from the southern bank. The bridge was a blazing inferno of dead bodies and blackened hulks. But more enemy vehicles were coming forward, and now the tanks left off their bombardment and began advancing down from the northern slopes above the river.

Geary's men, or what was left of them, came running back off the burning bridge. A tank made it to the northern end and came powering over the flaming concrete, knocking aside destroyed vehicles in its path. Willan had nothing left with which to stop it. Some of his men were running for the rear; only isolated groups were still holding out around their officers.

Something streaked past Willan's left shoulder and the tank on the bridge was rocked back by a massive explosion. The turret was blown off and went careering backwards.

He turned to look and saw a mass of vehicles halted on the ground behind the position. They were big American trucks, half-tracks and, absurdly, a small white civilian car. Men were jumping out of the trucks and running forward carrying boxes and weapons.

Morgan cannoned into him, a smoking RPG7 still on his shoulder. He looked amazingly clean to Willan. He was grinning.

'Better late than never, eh, Sarge?'

Willan was lost for words. He stared in dawning elation at the hundreds of men who were filing forward into his battered positions, all of them bearing ammo boxes, some carrying anti-tank weapons. Within a couple of minutes the fire from his side of the river increased five-fold, and anti-tank rounds were slamming into APCs and tanks on the northern bank.

The Ugandans began to pull back hurriedly, their infantry cut down by the dozen as they tried to rejoin their vehicles, the vehicles themselves scattering mud to all sides as they reversed frenziedly out of the killing zone. In moments the entire Ugandan formation was in full retreat, heading in a panicked crowd for the dead ground on the other side of the hills to the north. They left the northern bank of the Kagera littered with bodies and burning wrecks.

The firing tailed off. Even the tanks had ceased their bombardment. The silence was broken only by the crackle of flames and the groans of the wounded.

12

Willan drank deeply from the water bottle, trying to wash the filth and smoke reek out of his mouth. The exhaustion was like a weight of lead in his marrow. He could not remember ever feeling so tired, even on SBS selection.

He was standing to the rear of one of the trucks which had transported Morgan, Kigoma and the reinforcements from Mwanza. The vehicle's wheels had six inches of red mud on them and the windscreen wipers had carved solid Vs out of the dirt on the glass. Clearly, they had had a hard time getting here.

But not as hard a time as we had staying here, Willan thought vaguely. He drank from the water bottle again.

'We meet once more, Sergeant Willan,' a woman's voice said.

It was the Australian photojournalist.

'Aren't you going to say hello?'

What was her name? He couldn't remember – so much seemed to have happened since then.

'Hi,' he mumbled.

'I see you've been busy.'

Prentiss came up. Both he and the young woman seemed incredibly clean and alert. Willan had got used to the filth and blood and vermin that were an everyday fact of life in the bush. He knew he looked like three pounds of shit stuffed in a two-pound bag, but that did not matter – not now. He was alive, and they had won. They had held the bridge and beaten the Ugandans. For the moment. It was something to savour.

'Here,' the young woman said, and handed him a hip-flask. 'You look as though you could do with it.'

He unscrewed the top and drank. Whisky. It seared his throat and set up a glow in his gullet. His head seemed to clear.

'Thanks.' He handed it back. She smiled at him. Sue – that was her name. 'Thanks, Sue.'

'Oh, so you remember?'

'Sure.'

Prentiss was looking at the position Willan's men had fought and died for, particularly the two great bomb craters which dominated the centre of it. He whistled softly, the first time Willan could recall seeing him visibly impressed.

'How many of you are left?'

Willan wiped his face with one filthy hand. The sweat was cutting through the grime and stinging the small scratches and abrasions which covered his forehead and cheeks. He had not felt them before.

'We've got at least eighty wounded, as far as I can count. A lot of desertions, both on the withdrawal last night and when things looked pretty bad earlier today. I'd say we were down to about 150 effectives before the reinforcements turned up in the nick of time. Just like the bloody cavalry in a bad western. We'd have folded otherwise. We were at the end of our rope.'

'I believe you,' Prentiss murmured.

'I lost two of my own section, Tony Parker and Jock Fraser. They're lying somewhere on the road to the north.'

'I'm sorry,' Sue said.

'They took their chances, like the rest of us. Pity about their families, though. They'll probably never know just how and where they died.' Here Willan stared at Prentiss.

The MI6 man would not meet his eyes.

'What are you doing here anyway?' Willan asked Sue.

'I'm covering the war of course. I'm an official correspondent. The government here wants lots of pictures – evidence of Ugandan aggression.'

'Well, there's plenty of bodies to snap if you want to,' Willan said disgustedly. He turned away.

'Wait!' Prentiss said.

'What now?'

'Can your men hold the bridge for another day, Willan?'

The SBS sergeant looked at the crumbling, muddy trenches that the men were digging, the burial parties at work, the piles of bodies. While those who had been doing the fighting for the past two days rested, the fresh men under Morgan and Kigoma were rebuilding the crude defences and redistributing the reserve ammunition. Some were handing out boxes of rations which were being greedily consumed by the ragged, bloody scarecrows of soldiers who had had almost nothing to eat in two days.

'Who's asking?' Willan wanted to know.

'The government, let's say.'

'Well, if they don't launch a fresh armoured

attack, if they don't bomb us again, if we get more ammunition and food, then maybe. Why?'

'By tomorrow the first of the militias will be here to relieve your men, and ammunition will have been forwarded from Dodoma.'

'You mean we'll be taken out of the line?'

'Not all of you. Some of you.'

'What do you mean, Prentiss? I'm in no fucking mood for mind games.'

'All right. There may be another mission for your SBS men.'

'You mean you'll take us away from the battalion?'

'Yes. That part of your mission is accomplished, and accomplished well. Whitehall will be pleased.'

Willan laughed, and turned away.

'Well, fucking hooray,' he said.

The Ugandan Army seemed to be satisfied with its gains of the past two days. It had taken almost 800 square miles of Tanzanian soil at the cost of a crippled armoured regiment, and was now consolidating its gains. Though the men on the river saw the occasional Savarin on the skyline, the rest of the enemy were keeping a low profile for the moment, no doubt resting and refitting for the next attack.

The militias arrived the next morning in a fantastic assortment of vehicles. Civilian cars, trailer-pulling tractors, vans, trucks, even mopeds. There were hundreds of them, and they clogged up the road all the way back to Kyaka.

Most were armed with AK47s, some of them so new the preserving grease was still on them. They all carried spare magazines and bundles of food. They were without uniforms, most of them without shoes. They stared in wonder at the site of the previous day's battle, the burnt-out vehicles, the mass grave.

'Who the hell are they?' Willan asked as he watched them come in. They looked as carefree as schoolboys in a playground.

'Ugandans, most of them,' Okello told him. 'There are thousands like them in Tanzania, all exiles. These are only the youngest, the ones who want to fight back. They have seen now that the Ugandan Army is not invincible, so they have come to volunteer.'

'I take it you'll be in charge of them, Okello.'

'I believe so – they are my people, after all. You have done us all a very great service,

Colonel Willan. You have shown us how to fight. Now we have to go and reclaim our country.'

Fine talk, Willan thought, but he couldn't see these ragged, barefoot soldiers prevailing against the tanks and MiGs of Idi Amin. He did not say so, however.

'My men and I will be leaving you soon, I think,' he said instead.

'So I gathered. I believe that man Prentiss has a job for you to do elsewhere.'

'That's us, troubleshooters for hire,' Willan said with sour humour.

'Be careful, Colonel Willan.'

'I'm only a sergeant, you know. We're none of us officers – just grunts.'

Okello saluted him. 'In England, you may be a sergeant; here you are a colonel. You have earned the rank. Now if you will excuse me, sir, I must go and see to my men.'

He walked off, carrying himself as though he were on a parade ground, though he looked like a ragged vagabond, his once-immaculate uniform in stinking tatters. Willan watched him go, knowing he would miss Okello, and the battalion he had helped build up and whose baptism of fire he had taken part in.

Geary joined him.

'Prentiss is after us. He has a truck ready back on the road. He's ready to leave.'

'So soon?' Willan asked, surprised.

'He's been on the blower in Kyaka to some bigwigs in the government. Seems they require our presence urgently elsewhere.'

'Nice to be wanted,' Willan snarled.

'I've got the other lads together – what's left of them. What about Fraser and Parker's bodies, Sarge? Are they just going to be left there?'

Willan shrugged. 'There's not a hell of a lot we can do about it, Willy. Come on, let's not keep the spook waiting.'

'You all packed?' Geary asked him in a lighter tone.

Willan held up his AK47. 'I'm sending the other luggage separately.'

'Don't forget your dinner-jacket,' Geary retorted.

The pair of them made their way through the mob of newly arrived militiamen, leaving behind the position they had defended to such cost. The other SBS men were waiting on board a rickety, wooden-sided farm truck which stank of dung. Prentiss and Sue were in the cab.

'We're leaving in style, eh, Sarge?' Morgan called out cheerily.

Willan bent to the driver's window.

'Where are we going?' he asked Prentiss.

'Mwanza, for starters. You men could do with a cold beer and a bath.'

'I fucking second that,' Geary said with feeling.

'What about them?' Willan asked, gesturing to the defenders of the bridge and the men he had trained himself.

'They'll get by. Okello has been given overall command, and there are more militia units on the way, as well as some heavy equipment from Dodoma.'

'I don't like just walking away like this,' Willan said stubbornly.

'Believe me, Sergeant, what you are going to do next is the best way of helping them you could find.'

'Yeah, right,' Willan said. Then he raised his eyes to the sky. A drop of water hit him on the forehead. Then another. Soon the rain was falling more heavily, and the sky was becoming dark with grey cloud.

'Oh, great,' Morgan said from the back of the truck. 'Just on fucking schedule.'

'It could be worse,' Breckenridge quipped.

'You could be in one of those bloody trenches.'

Willan clambered into the back of the old pick-up truck without another word. Prentiss started the engine and pointed its nose south, against the flow of men on foot and other vehicles that were coming up the Kyaka road.

The rain began to come down in torrents, turning the road into a muddy red river. The back of the pick-up began to fill with water, to the weary disgust of the SBS men. Their battered vehicle bumped and lurched south, away from the war and the battlefields they had fought over. But Willan had a feeling they were not leaving the war behind. They would be back in it again soon enough, if Prentiss had his way.

He nodded off to sleep, the rain pouring down unheeded on his blackened face.

Willan was alone at the bar. Prentiss had booked them into the Deluxe Hotel again and, unbelievably, had come up with more garish civilian clothing for them all. The other SBS men were still in their rooms, sleeping. Willan had had a two-hour bath to soak out the dirt, but sleep was something that would not come to him. He kept thinking of the youngsters dug in along the Kagera, their trenches filling up with rain. He felt he had deserted them, and his dislike for the MI6 agent who had engineered his departure was rapidly intensifying into hatred. Several times during the day he had wondered what it would be like to punch Prentiss very hard on the nose.

Sue Morris entered the bar looking like the proverbial million dollars. She was wearing a long, flowery dress with bare arms and a low neckline. She looked tanned, fit, wholesome – as though she had just stepped out of the pages of a magazine. Memories of her well-toned body came back to Willan. A pity he had been so drunk; he could remember hardly anything from their encounter.

'I see your taste in shirts has not improved,' she said, taking a seat next to him.

'It's that bastard Prentiss. I think he does it just to piss me off.'

She held up a hand, cutting off further conversation. 'Turn it up, will you?' she asked the barman.

The barman dutifully turned up the volume on the flickering black and white television that was perched above the bar. Willan and Sue watched it in silence.

News of the war, for what it was worth. There was no footage of the actual fighting; no film crews had made it as far north as the Kagera salient yet. But there were still shots of the Kagera bridge with a destroyed T-55 in the middle of it, and the trenches on the south side of the river. A government spokesman said that Tanzanian forces, in conjunction with elements of exiled Ugandans, had halted the Ugandan invasion in its tracks and were now holding the Kagera in strength. President Nyerere appeared and promised that before the end of the year Ugandan troops would be expelled from every foot of Tanzanian territory, and that military units were being raised all over the country to that end. He warned his countrymen that they could be in for a protracted struggle.

Then, remarkably, Idi Amin appeared, interviewed in Kampala. He in turn promised that his army would press on south as soon as it had consolidated its gains, and he laughed off the suggestion that the Tanzanians would mount a counter-offensive soon. He reminded the interviewer that his country possessed the best army in East Africa, and that he had the support of the governments of Libya and Zaire, both of whom had promised to aid him militarily if he so desired. He poked fun at the Tanzanian forces and the Ugandan exiles, whom he called traitors to their country.

The programme ended with the news that Ugandan planes had heavily bombed the ports of Bukoba and Musoma and had also buzzed Mwanza. Willan knew that. He had seen a few ruined buildings on his way to the hotel in the back of Prentiss's commandeered truck. But at least the rains had now grounded the dictator's planes again.

'Turn it off, for fuck's sake,' Willan barked at the barman. Idi Amin's posturings had begun to wind him up. The worst thing was that everything he had said was true.

'Those shots of the Kagera bridge . . .' he said to his companion.

'Mine,' Sue replied smugly. 'A world exclusive. They've provided me with a tidy little nest-egg.'

'So why aren't you still up at the river, getting more?'

'Two reasons. Firstly, there's not much going on up there at the moment, and any shots I took would just be more of the same. Secondly, the world and his wife, in press terms, are now trekking north to be in on the action. I need a different angle.'

Light dawned on Willan at last. 'So that's why you're here. You think we may be able to get you another lead, another exclusive. And here was I thinking it was me you were after.'

'Business is business,' she said with a smile. 'Buy me a beer, Willan.'

He did so, noting her legs as she crossed them on the bar stool.

'I notice there was no mention of British soldiers in the news, no word on how it was a British-trained force which held up the invaders,' she said casually.

'We're not here,' Willan told her. 'I don't exist. You'd do well to remember that, reporter or not.'

'But *that* would be a story and a half, wouldn't it? How Tanzania, whose president hates all things colonial, had to ask the old colonial power for help in maintaining her borders.'

'You run a story like that, and you'll be out of this country before your feet touch the ground,' Willan told her. 'You'll piss off a whole world of people.'

'Including you?'

He turned on her.

'I don't give a flying fuck what you print or what you don't. My job is to fight, and to help others to fight. Two of my friends are already dead doing that; their bodies are lying unburied in the Kagera salient, along with hundreds of others. If you want to print something, then print that, but don't be fucking coy with me. I haven't the patience for it.'

She looked a little shocked. 'I'm sorry. I just didn't think . . .'

'Too fucking right you didn't. This country is fighting for its survival against one of the worst regimes the world has seen since the Nazis, and all you can think about is a little personal glory. Maybe that's your job to think that way, but it's not mine, and if you go plastering our existence all over the newspapers, then we'll be on the same plane out of here as you, and this country will be that little less able to defend itself. So be a good girl, eh? Do as you're told; think like a human being for once, instead of a fucking newshound.'

She glared at him, obviously furious. God, she's pretty, Willan found himself thinking.

'At least I'm not a cold-blooded killer,'

she hissed, then turned and flounced out of the bar.

Shit. Now why did he do that? Why the high-horsed speech? He'd never get another roll in the hay with her now.

Willan ordered another beer. The barman smiled at him sympathetically.

'Women, eh?' Willan said. 'Can't live with them, can't live with them. Cheers.' He sank the cold beer gratefully.

The SBS men, sweet-smelling, refreshed and stuffed with their first decent meal in days, met in Prentiss's hotel room. It looked like a tasteless shirt convention, Willan thought. He was angry at himself because he had had too many beers at a time when his mind should be clear, and he was still annoyed at having mouthed off to Sue like that. He did not like to hear people preach, and he had given her quite a sermon.

Prentiss unrolled a map of Lake Victoria and its shores and weighted it down with beer bottles. The six surviving SBS men crowded round it.

'We have a mission for you,' Prentiss said, puffing on one of his reeking cigarettes.

'Who's *we*?' Morgan asked.

'Never mind. There is a target, or rather a series of targets, that we need taken out ASAP.' The MI6 agent stabbed a finger down on the map.

'Here.'

'Entebbe,' Willan said. He experienced an odd sinking feeling.

'Just so. We want you to raid the airport at Entebbe . . .'

'What, like the Israelis did a couple of years ago?' Gordon asked.

'Not quite. This time there are no hostages. The objectives are the sixty or so aircraft which are stationed there. Your job will be to disable or destroy as many of them as you can while they are still on the ground.'

Breckenridge whistled softly. 'Sixty! That's ten apiece – a tall order if ever there was one.'

'It's been calculated that if you can take out half of them then you will have reduced the air threat facing the Tanzanians to acceptable proportions.'

'I'd love to know who works out all these things,' Willan said drily.

'The air threat,' Prentiss went on, ignoring him, 'is the single thing which is most capable of breaking the back of Tanzanian resistance.

226

We can't allow the bombing of Tanzanian towns to go on any longer, to say nothing of the harm airstrikes can do to the infantry on the ground.'

'We have some experience of that,' Hill said archly.

'Quite.' Prentiss pulled out another map, smaller this time. It seemed to be the map of a long, narrow peninsula.

'Here we have the Entebbe peninsula. You see that the airport is near its tip. There are two main runways, the southern and the south-western. Between the V formed by these runways are the main military hangars. Some of the targets are in these hangars. Look east. Closer to the eastern shore of the promontory are a series of taxi-ways and concrete holding areas. There are also large fuel tanks.'

'Aha,' Morgan said happily.

'Yes. About two-thirds of the Ugandan Air Force is parked within a couple of hundred yards of the tanks – it's because they don't have enough refuelling vehicles; it's more convenient that way.'

'You're implying that if we take out the tanks, then the planes will be destroyed with them,' Willan said.

'Many of them will, yes. But there will have

to be charges placed on the aircraft also, just
in case. The Ugandans don't drain the fuel
tanks of the aircraft themselves after every
flight and quite a few of those planes will
still have high-octane fuel in them, so they'll
go up like torches. We need two teams: one
to set the charges on the main fuel tanks,
another to set explosives on as many aircraft as
possible which are farthest away from the tanks
themselves, to add to the general effect.'

'How many aircraft would that take out, if
all went according to plan?' Willan asked.

'We think between thirty and forty.'

'Nice one,' Gordon said.

'What about security?' Geary wanted to
know.

'Lax. They have a decaying perimeter
fence: barbed wire and the like. There is a
guardroom between the two runways housing
about a platoon of troops, and they have
several jeeps armed with fifty-cal Brownings
which patrol somewhat erratically the entire
airfield.'

'Not so good,' Willan said. 'I'd rather we
had well-disciplined troops who kept to a nice,
predictable schedule.'

'They are inefficient in the extreme,' Prentiss
said. 'An attack on Entebbe is the last thing

they expect. You will have the advantage of total surprise.'

'How do we get there?' Hill asked. 'It's all the way across Lake Victoria.'

Prentiss smiled. 'Remember that big white boat you captured? Well, it's still where you cached it, and your canoes and other maritime equipment are on board.'

'You've got to be kidding,' Willan said.

'I'm not.'

'But we'd be a sitting duck in that thing – their air force could blow us out of the water any time they liked.'

'Not in weather like this,' Prentiss said, gesturing out of the hotel room window to where the torrential rain was still pouring down outside.

'And if it stops raining again?' Morgan asked.

'We will move by night. The drop-off point for the canoes will be west of Kkome Island, six miles offshore. You'll paddle in, do the business and then paddle out again.'

'Simple,' Willan said sardonically. 'You'll be piloting the boat, will you?'

'Yes, since my talent seems to run that way. And a crew of Ugandan exiles is being given to us, some of whom are natives of the Ssese

Islands. They know those waters like their own backyards.'

'You say all our gear is intact and on the steamer?' Willan asked.

'Yes.'

Willan sighed. 'All right. Let's get down to brass tacks. Timings . . .'

The other SBS men looked at one another. The operation was on. They brought out notebooks and began taking down the orders which would take them north into Uganda.

13

The rain hitting the surface of the lake sounded like sausages sizzling in a pan. Willan peered out of the streaming windows of the wheelhouse at the darkness beyond. It was a moonless night, six days after the hotel-room briefing. The surface of Lake Victoria was flat and even; there was no wind to speak of either, which suited him fine.

Visibility was down to about three hundred yards on account of the rain, and the old steamer was powering along with all lights out except the little glow which illuminated the binnacle. Prentiss was standing at the engine controls while a Ugandan native, Ukune, steered the ship. Down in the engine-room another group of Ugandan exiles were stoking up the boilers to keep a good head of steam going. The *Victoria* was making twelve knots; almost flat out for her.

They had left the little cove near Mwanza the evening before, and had lain up during the following day in the shelter of the tiny, uninhabited island of Nabuyongo. Now they were in Ugandan waters. Off to their left was the tangled archipelago of the Ssese Islands. Their course was west-north-west, designed to bring them just to the left of Kkome. The drop-off point was only two hours away now, and the other SBS men were on deck, readying their equipment.

They would take the Kleppers in on the approach. The Rigid Raiders were too large and it would be too risky to use their engines. The six SBS men would paddle in silently, the two strongest, Morgan and Breckenridge, towing two unmanned canoes behind them filled with extra limpet mines.

The section would then split into three groups. Hill would stay with the canoes on the shore and do his best to make sure that any Ugandan sentry who stumbled upon them did not live long enough to boast about it. Geary and Breckenridge would set off for the fuel tanks a few hundred yards away, setting charges on each one. And the largest group, composed of Willan, Morgan and Gordon, would have the most dangerous task. They would have to travel farther still and place limpet mines on as many as possible of the aircraft which were parked on the taxi-ways of the southern runway.

Once the charges were in place, everyone would leg it back to the canoes and then paddle like hell for the old steamer which would be waiting six miles offshore. Once they were in the water, Willan had ordered them not to stop for anyone or anything. Anyone who was discovered was to make as big a fight of it as possible to gain the others time to get away.

Or, Willan thought grimly to himself, as much fight as one man could put up when he was in a flimsy canoe. He still had that odd sinking feeling about the whole operation. It was another typical seat-of-the-pants job, as everything else had been in Africa.

The SBS were armed with their Ingrams again, all fitted with silencers, and shoulder-holstered Brownings. They would wear tropical diving suits, but no fins, and would carry with them an assortment of grenades and flares as well as the explosives essential to the success of the mission. Once they had rejoined the steamer, Prentiss would take the old ship into the labyrinth of the Ssese Islands to lie up all the next day and avoid pursuit. It was known that the Ugandans had a few ageing patrol boats based at Port Bell, some twenty miles from Entebbe, and it would be as well to avoid them if they were called out, rather than try to batter a course through them.

'We're at the drop-off point,' Prentiss said at last, consulting the ship's compass and his watch. He clanged the engine levers back and forth.

'All stop.'

The engines faded to a murmur and the ship lost way. The night became almost silent.

He and Willan went out on deck. The SBS men, with the help of the Ugandan crew, were already lowering the Kleppers over the side, and then sliding down the ropes after them. It was all done in near silence, only the dull thuds of the canoes bumping against the steel hull of the steamer breaking the quiet of the night. That, and the endless rain.

Willan smeared cam cream thickly over his face and hands and hitched the Ingrams higher on his shoulder. His canoe was already in the water. He took hold of the rope.

'Good luck,' Prentiss said, holding out a hand.

Willan shook it. 'You'll stay on station until four-thirty?'

'Yes, as we arranged. After that I'll be lying off Bubeke Island in the Ssese archipelago. Break a leg, Willan.'

'I probably will,' Willan muttered. He slid easily down the rope, his rubber-clad feet thumping lightly against the steamer's hull. There was an awkward moment as he levered himself into the bobbing Klepper, but then he was in, his paddle in his hands, the other canoes about him. There was no hint of brightness or shine about the other canoeists; they merged with the night completely.

'Let's go, lads,' Willan whispered, and he dug his paddle into the rain-pocked lake.

It was easy going, despite the rain. The tricky part was the navigation. Willan was consulting his wrist compass every few hundred yards, keeping them on the bearing that would take them to their landing point.

The eight canoes made good time. Despite being burdened with another of the Kleppers to tow behind each of them, Morgan and Breckenridge kept up easily with the others. The lake itself was empty at this time of night and in this weather. Even had there been boats out on the water, they would never have noticed the silent little vessels which glided along in their midst; the SBS had made water-borne penetration into a fine art.

Muscles which Willan had not used in weeks were beginning to ache a little when he finally saw the tell-tale lights of the shore up ahead, blurred in the rain. The airfield, Prentiss had assured them, was not well illuminated beyond the lights of the runways and the tower. There were very few commercial flights in or out of Uganda these days. Europeans had been discouraged from visiting the country for the past five years, since Amin had seized a number of white tourists and accused them of spying back in 1974. And then, of course, there had been the Entebbe raid, two years before, when Israeli commandos had stormed the airport to liberate a group of Jewish hostages from Amin's clutches.

Willan began scanning the shoreline. He was looking for a dent in the coast, a tiny bay to the west of the airport which Prentiss had assured him would be an ideal insertion point.

He saw it, and adjusted course minutely. The other canoes followed him without question. Geary would be check-navigating at the rear.

The lights seemed very close now, throwing bars of brightness across the lake. This was one of the worst parts: the possibility of being seen while they were still relatively helpless out on the water.

Willan's canoe bumped lightly against sand. He stepped out of it and grabbed the short tow-rope at its prow. With his free hand he held the Ingrams at the ready. The weapon was loaded and cocked. He began wading ashore in calf-deep water, towing the Klepper behind him.

The canoe's bottom scraped on dry sand. He hauled it entirely out of the water, then took up position on his belly near the top of a nearby sand-dune. In seconds the rest of the team were all around him. They spread out in a horseshoe, the open end of the formation resting on the lake, and lay there without a word, watching and waiting.

Nothing. The airport was clearly visible now. There were a few cars moving on the road to its north-east end, travelling up to Kampala perhaps. Willan could see almost everything: the fuel tanks, great metallic cylinders almost directly ahead, and beyond them, lines and lines of parked planes: MiG 16s and 17s, and a few Pucára ground-attack aircraft.

He saw a sentry strolling along among the planes. He made out the guardroom, the jeeps with their Brownings parked outside. The place seemed sleepy, almost deserted.

He tapped Gordon and Morgan on the shoulder. They nodded at him and then began dishing out limpet mines. Breckenridge was doing the same. The SBS men placed them in canvas shoulder bags which rode at both hips. They were heavy and awkward, and if a man moved suddenly they would clink together; but it could not be helped – not now.

Willan's team moved out first, as they had the farthest to go. Next came Geary and Breckenridge. Hill remained behind, watching.

Beyond the dunes the ground dipped and became marshy. It was thick with reeds, which made for agonizingly slow progress. Willan's team threaded their way through the stems as quietly as they could, their feet sucking in the mud and water underfoot. Luckily, the rain continued to pour down, covering them with a blanket of sound. They had to pause once to let a water snake slither by. At least seven feet long, it sidled out in front of Willan with its head held up out of the mud. It seemed to pause and regard him for a moment, then slithered away. Willan unfroze. He was sweating, moisture stinging his eyes as the rain washed it off his forehead. Victoria's water snakes possessed some of the deadliest venom in the world. The SBS men had been told before they left England that the tropical suits would protect them from snake bite, but he had no wish to put his to the test.

They reached the end of the reeds at last and went down on their bellies in the foul-smelling ooze. There was a short expanse of open ground, now slimy with mud and full of puddles, and then the fence of the airfield itself. It was an ordinary wire fence with a coil of Dannet wire at its top and bottom.

Willan tapped Gordon on the shoulder and the SBS man moved out while the other two covered him, alert for any sign of movement nearby. Further to the south, Geary and Breckenridge would also be on the move now. The two teams were taking separate approach routes to maximize their chances of evading discovery.

Gordon was lying at the foot of the fence plying the wire-cutters. Thank God for the rain, Willan thought. It screened most small sounds and made the sentries perfunctory in their duties.

Small, metallic sounds came from the fence. Willan nodded at Morgan and the big man went over to help Gordon, holding the wire taut while the wire-cutters severed it, so that it would not spring up.

They were through. There was a gap perhaps eighteen inches wide in the wire now and Gordon was squirming through it. Morgan followed, then the pair took up fire positions on the other side. There was very little cover save for the darkness and the rain. Willan splashed over to the fence and crawled through. One of the canvas bags holding the limpet mines snagged on an end of wire, and he had to pause for what seemed like an age and free himself. He was through, thank Christ.

They rearranged the wire so that at a casual glance it would look undisturbed. Then Willan stopped to plant a four-inch twig upright in the ground by the breach so they would be able to find their exit on the return journey.

They moved on. The fuel tanks were to their left now but their own objective was farther away: the lines of planes parked adjacent to the southern runway.

Willan threw himself to the ground.

There was a jeep rumbling up the runway itself, headlights blazing. He closed one eye to preserve his night vision. Behind him, Gordon and Morgan lay as still as statues.

The jeep rumbled past barely eighty yards away, illuminating twin cones of falling rain as it went. Willan started breathing again.

They got to their feet and continued, only to pause and go to ground again two minutes later. There was the glow of a cigarette in the darkness. A man was standing there smoking, his hand protecting the cigarette from the rain. They saw his face illuminated in the tiny red glow for a second as he dragged on it. He wore a bush hat and his rifle was slung on his shoulder.

Willan turned and gave the thumbs down, meaning 'enemy', to the others. Then he pointed to himself and made a chopping motion with his hand, telling them he was going to take him out. He saw Gordon and Morgan nod, then moved into a crouch with the silenced Ingrams held high. He clicked the selector to single shot and began padding towards the smoking sentry as silently as a cat.

Closer, closer. He distrusted the accuracy of the stubby little sub-machine-gun and wanted to get as near as possible to the target.

Twenty yards, fifteen.

Willan's foot slid in mud. He staggered, and the mines in his shoulder bags clanked together.

The sentry turned, and caught sight of the dark figure stalking him, barely forty feet away.

Willan raised the Ingrams and fired. There was a low thump, a minute spark of flame from the muzzle, and the sentry was hurled backwards to land on his back in the mud.

The bullet had taken him squarely in the chest; visibility was too bad for Willan to have tried for a head shot and he had not wanted to risk a 'double-tap' because of the noise. The man was gurgling, still moving.

Willan was on him in a flash. He dropped his weapon to its sling and whipped out his knife from the thigh scabbard. He held one hand over the man's mouth and slit his throat from ear to ear. He held the sentry down as the man thrashed about frantically. But his struggles did not last long, and when he was completely still, Willan resheathed the knife and took up the Ingrams again, listening. He could feel the blood on his face; the man's jugular had spouted like a hose.

Nothing. He clicked his fingers three times and Gordon and Morgan joined him. They grabbed the body and the AK47, which had fallen from his shoulder. They popped the still-smoking cigarette in the man's open mouth. It hissed in blood.

There were a series of shacks nearby, down beside the runway – probably maintenance sheds. They hid the body behind one of them and paused to listen again.

A jeep engine in the distance. Patrolling the other runway perhaps. The night was quiet but for the continual hiss of the rain and the faint, far-off rumble of nocturnal traffic on the Kampala road.

The aircraft were just in front of them, shining in the wet. Willan consulted his watch, lifting off the cover to peer at the luminous dial. They were behind schedule. He gave the thumbs up to the other two men and then the team split up, each one of them moving like a shadow to his own designated area of operation.

They would place a mine on every third plane. The limpets were compact but powerful and if, as Prentiss had assured them, there was still fuel in the aircraft's tanks, then it should prove easy enough to cripple nearby planes as well as the mined ones.

The limpets were fixed so as to go off at set times, and all of them were staggered so that they would explode in a series, for maximum confusion. They were also arranged so that Geary and Breckenridge's charges on the fuel tanks would go off first, hopefully spraying this area of the field with blazing high-octane fuel. The ensuing fireball should be impressive, to say the least.

Willan clicked the first mine into place under the fuselage of a MiG 16, then twisted the cap to arm it, and pressed in the timer. It could just be heard ticking.

He moved on to the next aircraft, watching and listening constantly for signs of the enemy. No problem. This area of the field was silent as a grave; the Ugandans were either incredibly confident or unforgivably lax.

'This is for Jock,' Willan murmured as he clicked the second mine into place. 'This is for Parker,' he said for the third. 'And this is from me, you cunts,' as he clicked the fourth and last into place.

He was done.

Just then he heard the roar of a vehicle engine

accelerating nearby, and immediately after, the shockingly loud sound of heavy-calibre machine-gun fire ripping the night apart.

Willan ran swiftly though the maze of planes towards the bright flare of automatic fire that was flashing down by the runway. There was a jeep there, its occupants manning a fifty-calibre Browning and blasting off rounds for all they were worth.

He saw tracer bouncing off tarmac, zooming all over the night sky. There was a shadow ducking in among the parked aircraft much as he was himself. Was it Gordon or Morgan?

Return fire, the low thumping of a silenced Ingrams. Willan crept under the wing of a plane, looking for a fire position.

There. Got you, you bastards.

He opened up on the jeep, spraying it with an entire magazine. The three occupants were thrown about like dolls, one hurled off the vehicle entirely. The firing stopped.

There was the high whine of a siren, like an old anti-aircraft warning. Willan could hear other vehicle engines starting, men shouting in confusion. It sounded as though they had disturbed the Ugandans' beauty sleep.

'Thanks, Sarge. The fucker came out of

nowhere with his lights off, just coasting down the runway. Caught me napping.'

It was Gordon.

'Where's Mick?'

'Here,' another voice said, and the massive figure of Morgan came hulking out of the darkness.

'The shit's hit the fan now. Time to fuck off. All charges placed?' Willan asked.

The other two men nodded.

'Let's grab the jeep then. Mick, man the Browning. Gordy, you drive.'

They threw off the two bodies still on the vehicle and Gordon gunned the engine, then sped off, kicking up dirt with the spinning rear wheels. Behind them, the whole airfield was coming alive with running men and roaring vehicles, but the pursuit was as yet uncoordinated. Hopefully, they'd mistake the jeep for one of their own.

Automatic fire stitched the ground to their left. A crowd of Ugandan soldiers were rattling along to one side in an old truck, leaning their elbows on the cab and firing as they came. Gordon spun the jeep off to the right while Morgan swung the heavy Browning and got off a burst which made the other vehicle skid and swerve in the wet ground.

'So much for mistaken identity,' Willan growled, and lobbed off a phosphorus grenade behind them to complicate matters for the opposition.

There was a flash up ahead, followed by a roaring boom as the charges on the fuel tanks went up. Geary and Breckenridge had done their job at any rate. Another flash, the thunder of another detonation. The eastern sky became filled with a sheet of flame a hundred feet high. Burning high-octane fuel was flung though the air and splashed in blazing torrents over the southern runway and the planes parked beside it. Gordon swung the jeep crazily to the left to avoid the flames. The entire night was a vast furnace of light and secondary explosions.

'We're cut off, Sarge!' Gordon yelled. 'The whole fucking eastern perimeter is on fire!'

'Head north,' Willan told him. In the back, Morgan was firing burst after burst of heavy-calibre rounds at their pursuers.

More explosions, from the rows of parked planes this time. Willan saw a wing blasted into the air, tailplanes thrown across the runway.

'Holy shit!' Prentiss had been right: there had indeed been fuel left in the aircraft. Detonation after detonation went off in sequence, causing havoc, spraying wreckage and burning petrol for hundreds of yards around the airfield. They could feel the heat of the fires like the African sun heating their faces.

Three other jeeps behind them, their on-board weapons twinkling with muzzle flashes. The noise of the fires and the explosions was too great for Willan to hear the gunfire.

A geyser of earth blew up on one side of the jeep. Gravel sliced into Willan's wetsuit and tore the flesh over one eye.

'Fuck! What was that?'

Morgan shouted an answer.

'They've got a couple of M-79s on those jeeps. They're ranging in on us, Sarge!' He gritted his teeth and laid down a storm of heavy fire to their rear. One jeep caught the full impact of a dozen rounds. The driver was cut almost in two. He slumped over the wheel and the vehicle skidded, slid and toppled over on one side, spinning round and scattering its occupants until it came to rest with its wheels spinning lazily in the air. Morgan whooped.

'One for the good guys!'

Then a burst of fire caught him across the chest and blasted him into the front seat. He landed almost on Willan's lap.

'Mick! Fuck! Step on it, Gordy. Evade that fucking fire.'

'How is he?'

Morgan's eyes were open in surprise. His chest had taken three rounds; half of his back had been blown away by the exit wounds. Willan closed the blood-filled eyes.

'He's dead, Gordy.'

They roared along without speaking. Willan clambered into the back. There was no ammunition left for the Browning.

'They're closing in to the front, Sarge,' Gordon told him. The jeep lurched and bumped over the uneven ground. To their right, the perimeter of the airfield was still a sea of flames.

'Head for the fence,' Willan told him. 'Try and burst through. We're fucked now, anyway.'

Gordon wrenched the wheel round and the jeep arced to the right, the offside wheels leaving the ground for a second. Tracer sped over Willan's head. He fired back with the Ingrams, but he was almost out of ammo for that too.

'Here we go!' Gordon yelled.

Fire all about them, flames taking away Willan's breath. The skin of his face was seared by the heat.

Then there was a crash. They impacted with

the perimeter fence and went right through it. The wire and posts swept over them, tearing through the windscreen, ripping the Browning from its mount. Gordon was knocked out of the driving seat and landed in the back with Willan. The jeep careered on, the tyres on fire now, rotating circles of flame.

The vehicle hit a bank. The nose thudded hard, throwing Willan and Gordon forward again; then it zoomed up into the air. There was a moment of weightlessness, followed by a horrendous crash, and they came to a halt.

Flames all about them. Gordon was unconscious, something sticking out the front of his wetsuit. Willan grabbed him and hauled him from the burning vehicle. He staggered through the fire and found himself walking though reeds, with mud and water sucking at his calves. His wetsuit was on fire, as was Gordon's. He flopped down among the reeds, dragging his comrade with him. The cooling water put out the flames. He felt rather than heard the jeep explode. Before him, sand-dunes were pale and firelit down to the sea.

'Gordy.'

But Gordon was dead. A post from the perimeter fence had transfixed him through the heart like a spear.

'Oh, Christ,' Willan groaned.

He took Gordon's spare magazines, then lurched away, loading his Ingrams. The entire sky behind him was a wall of flame; it looked like the end of the world. There were still explosions going off in the airfield, but none of his pursuers had dared to follow him through the flames. The beach before him was deserted. He reckoned he was almost a mile north of the insertion point.

Willan walked out into the water, checking behind him for pursuit. There was none. He blew into the buoyancy bags on the shoulders of his suit, and struck out into the lake. The water seemed very cold, but it was welcome on his seared skin. His eyebrows and eyelashes were gone, and it was agony to hold on to his weapon; he could see skin falling from his fingers in white folds.

When he was at least three hundred yards out from the shore he looked back, puffing. The coast was a line of yellow and orange flame. He could see nothing beyond the inferno. Well, they had done a fucking good job of eliminating the Ugandan Air Force. He wondered if Geary and Breckenridge had made it.

He swam as quickly as he could southwards, consulting his wrist compass as he went. After a while he found he could no longer hold on to the Ingrams: his fingers were too swollen and painful. He dropped it, his only weapons now the Browning High Power and his sheath knife.

Time went by endlessly. He was incredibly tired. It would be so easy to give up, to lie there and drift peacefully under the stars. But he kept going.

When he thought he had reached the approximate latitude of the insertion point, he dug out his pencil torch from his wetsuit pocket and began flashing it towards the shore. Bloody silly thing to do, but he was near the end of his rope. He could swim no farther. Besides, hopefully the Ugandans wouldn't notice such a tiny light out in the lake since they had such great fuck-off illumination on the shore to ruin their vision.

More time went by. The pain in his hands and face came and went in great sickening waves. He shut Morgan and Gordon out of his mind. Time enough to grieve later. For now he had to concentrate on survival.

Was there something out on the water? A splash of foam perhaps. He prayed it was not a curious crocodile. They were not common in this part of the lake, but that would just be the last straw.

Definitely something there. He thought he saw shapes backlit by the inferno of the coast. He blinked the little torch on and off.

Men in canoes. He grinned wearily. Fucking A.

That looked like Willy Geary in front. He'd know that little runt anywhere.

'Sarge?' Geary's voice asked. The paddling stopped.

'Yes,' Willan croaked. 'Give us a hand, for fuck's sake.'

The canoes came to a halt on either side of him. There were three of them. So Geary's team had made it, and Hill too. Thank God.

Someone grabbed his arm and hauled him up across the bow of the canoe. He cried out in pain, feeling blisters bursting under the wetsuit.

'Sarge, you all right? Where are the others?'

'They're dead, Willy. And I'm fucked. Get us the hell out of here.'

Without another word, Geary began paddling again. Willan's weight kept the bow of the Klepper low in the water, slowing them down.

'Any pursuit?' he asked at last when the pain had died down a little.

'No. I think they were all chasing you lot up to the north. We waited as long as we could. We sank the spare Kleppers offshore.'

'You did a good job, Willy.'

'How did Mick and Gordy get it?'

'We went through the flames and the fence. Mick got shot. Gordy got it in the crash. It was a massive fuck-up. They were all over us.'

'They were good lads,' Geary said quietly, paddling on like a machine. Willan could just hear the dip and splash of the other paddles. Hill and Breckenridge had drawn closer to listen.

'We'll be late for the RV with Prentiss. Think he'll hang around?' Geary asked.

'He'd better, or I'll fucking shoot him myself,' Willan snarled. Then he clenched his teeth, fighting the pain of his burns. He bent his forehead into the cool waters of the lake and closed his eyes.

14

Prentiss was nervous. He had heard the explosions to the north, and had subsequently seen the sky light up orange and red all along the horizon, like an early sunrise. So the mission was accomplished. That was something. But the SBS were over an hour late for the rendezvous, and it would be dawn very soon. If he was to get the steamer back in the shelter of the Ssese Islands before daylight he would have to leave in the next few minutes. The Ugandan Air Force might or might not be crippled by the raid, but Amin still had patrol boats based fairly close by, and the old steamer wasn't built for speed.

He raged at himself for coming along on this damn-fool trip. He was an intelligence gatherer, not a 'hot' operative. He had let his absurd sense of adventure and, if truth be told, the pleasure of captaining this antique boat, override his common sense. He should have given one of the men basic instructions on piloting the ship and awaited the turn of events in a bar in Mwanza.

But he was here now, and he had a decision to make. Just how much longer should he remain on station, endangering the lives of the crew and himself, waiting for the return of men who might be dead even as he stood here in the wheelhouse? He'd give it a few more minutes at any rate.

'Is the masthead light on?' he asked Ukune, the helmsman.

'Yes, skipper. Turned it on myself over an hour ago. How much longer will we wait, skipper?'

'As long as it takes,' Prentiss said with more resolve than he felt.

He began wondering what kind of diplomatic ramifications there would be if Amin found out that British soldiers had been helping out the Tanzanian government with a little sabotage. It would hurt Nyerere's standing with his neighbours, possibly damage the war effort. It would not be an easy job to convince the world that soldiers as well-trained and efficient as the SBS were in fact nothing more than mercenaries.

'The hell with it,' he said at last. 'Let's get out of here. They've had it.'

'No, skipper – I see something out there.'

'Where?'

'Off the port bow, maybe a hundred yards. Something is moving.'

Prentiss went out on deck and peered into the darkness. There was a glow on the eastern horizon now, but that was the sun coming up, not the inferno that the SBS had made of the Ugandan coastline.

A tiny wink of light, off and on at regular intervals. He let out a deep breath.

'That's them,' he called back to Ukune. 'Get the engine-room to make steam. We'll be moving out in a few minutes.' And not before time, he thought.

Three canoes, one with a body draped across its bow. They had taken casualties then. The canoes had halted at the ship's side, by the scramble net.

'Throw down a line!' someone said. 'We've got a casualty here.'

Prentiss called out for the deck crew. Three Ugandan exiles appeared and fed a rope down to the canoeists. There was a smell of burnt rubber which intensified as a body was hauled up on deck by the rope.

Willan. He was almost unrecognizable, his face a mass of burns. The wetsuit looked as though it had melted to his skin in places. Prentiss almost gagged at the smell.

'You waited then, you fucker,' Willan whispered. 'Just as well for you.' He closed his eyes.

'Take him below,' Prentiss ordered the deck-hands.

The other SBS men were appearing over the ship's side. They also smelt of burning, and petrol and cordite. Prentiss wondered what kind of hell they had been through. They looked ten years older.

'Get the masthead light off,' Geary said sharply. 'There are patrol boats out on the lake. They passed by us less than half an hour ago.'

'Right,' Prentiss heard himself saying. For once, he felt a little out of his depth.

The Kleppers were hauled up on deck and the SBS men peeled themselves out of their stinking wetsuits. The steamer got under way and began moving with all her lights off. There was the distant churn of her propellers, the rumble of her engines, but no other sound on the lake. It was getting brighter by the moment.

Geary and the other survivors were taking up position on the bows of the steamer, setting out spare magazines and looking as though they were preparing to fight another battle.

'What happened to the other two?' Prentiss asked.

'Dead,' Geary said curtly.

'But you accomplished the mission? You got the planes?'

'Yes. The mission was a complete success except that Mick and Gordy didn't make it. Any more questions?'

'No. I . . .'

'Set course for Bukoba. We're not stopping in the Ssese Islands. Willan needs a hospital, and there are no planes worth speaking of left intact at Entebbe.'

'But the patrol boats . . .'

'You let us worry about those. Just get this tub of shit back to Tanzania. Do it.'

Prentiss started to argue, but something in Geary's eyes stopped him. He had a momentary feeling that the SBS corporal would have as soon shot him on the spot as talk any further.

He went into the wheelhouse, adjusted their course and brought the *Victoria* up to full speed. If there were no interruptions, they would make Bukoba in about ten hours.

*   *   *

It became a beautifully clear day. The clouds had cleared and the rain of the previous night had died away. They could see for miles over the surface of the lake.

Fishing boats dotted the water – even in time of war, people had to eat. The sunlight glittered off the lake so that Prentiss had to shade his eyes from the glare. He had not slept or sat down all night, and he felt exhausted. And he would have to pilot this thing all the way to Tanzania now. The thought made him feel even more tired.

Geary entered the wheelhouse. He was stripped down to a grimy pair of shorts and wore a scorched set of webbing on his bare torso. The Ingrams dangled from one hand.

'How is Willan?'

'Sleeping,' Prentiss told him. 'I gave him a shot of morphine. He'll be out for hours.'

'Good. It's going to get a little noisy soon.'

'What do you mean?'

'There are two Ugandan patrol boats astern of us and closing fast.'

'Shit!' Prentiss hissed. He turned over the helm to a yawning Ukune and ran down the length of the steamer.

Breckenridge and Hill had moved to the stern and were kneeling behind the steel of the ship's rail and sighting down the barrels of their weapons. Prentiss could make out the dark shapes of the pursuers less than a mile astern, foam billowing up from their bows. They were gaining fast.

Geary joined him.

'We lost them last night, but they must have been quartering the lake ever since, and now it's daylight they've picked us up again.'

'What are we going to do?' Prentiss asked.

Geary smiled. 'Fight. What do you think? Tell me about these boats, Mr Intelligence agent.'

Prentiss collected his thoughts hurriedly.

'They're based on the hulls of old Second World War PT boats. They're fast, and I think they're armed with a couple of heavy-calibre machine-guns; that's all.'

'More sodding Brownings, I'll bet,' Breckenridge said disgustedly. He spat into the steamer's wake.

'You're sure they have nothing heavier?' Geary asked.

'Positive. And they're not too well run from what I've heard.'

'Good. Now you get back to driving the

boat, and we'll do our best to make them fuck off.'

Prentiss returned to the wheelhouse. There was little else for him to do.

Willan opened his eyes and groaned. Even that simple movement was painful. But he was alive, and the pain was not as bad as it had been.

A steel bulkhead above him; he must be on the steamer. So they had made it. He seemed to remember being hoisted aboard, but it was all very vague, like a dream.

He sat up, clenching his teeth against the pain. They must have given him a shot of something; he felt like he was a little drunk.

His arms and hands were heavily bandaged, but he could still flex his fingers. His face felt like a raw piece of meat. He had a feeling he'd not be too handsome once this little escapade was over. But he was alive, and that was something. Something more than Parker or Jock or Mick or Gordy had at any rate. Poor bastards.

He got up. He was dressed in shorts, nothing else, and smelt like a cross between a cesspool and a scrapyard.

Small-arms fire from up on deck. A series of

single shots, then a long rattle of automatic. He heard the roar of powerful engines out beyond the hull of the old steamer. That was what had woken him then.

He left the cabin and made his way up on deck.

Two long patrol boats were circling the steamer like Indians galloping round a wagon train. The backwash from their passage created a crazy series of foaming waves which made the *Victoria* dip and lurch as though she were in the midst of a heavy sea. Heavy-calibre fire was hitting the hull – a peculiar ringing sound.

Willan limped over to where the three SBS were crouching and returning fire.

'What's the score, Willy?' he asked his corporal.

'Sarge, you're supposed to be below.'

'I know. Spare me – tell me what they've got.'

'One fifty-cal, surprise surprise, and a shitload of small arms. Most of it's going wild, though, and this boat is a tough old bird, good Tyneside steel, 1914 vintage.'

'But it won't stop a fifty-cal. They can stand off and riddle us like a colander if they've a mind to.'

'I know. But there's not a lot we can do

with these,' said Geary, patting the Ingrams.
'And we're low on ammo too.'

'Think they'll try to board?'

'They had men all over their decks. I think
they will, yes; they're daft enough.'

'Those are old PT boats, aren't they?'

'That's right, like something out of an old
Pacific War film.'

'Then their lower hulls should be of wood,
so they don't set off mines.'

'I suppose so, Sarge.'

Geary threw himself flat on the deck as
a rattle of enemy fire strafed the vessel's
superstructure.

'They're moving in!' Hill yelled, firing off
short bursts of fire at the attackers.

Breckenridge and Geary began firing too.
One of the enemy boats had zoomed in close
and now a veritable barrage of small-arms
fire was storming the length of the steamer.
The wheelhouse was riddled and Ukune was
hurled back from the helm as a burst of rounds
exploded through his torso. The gauges and
instruments were shattered, and the *Victoria*
slewed round, out of control. Prentiss crawled
to the helm and tried to bring her back on
course. There was a great crash as the steamer
collided with the smaller enemy vessel on her

port side. Some of the Ugandans leapt off their vessel and clung to the scramble net, which was still hanging down the ship's side. They began pulling themselves upwards while fire from their comrades in the patrol boats kept the heads of the SBS down.

The Ugandans were over the ship's rail now, running along the deck and firing wildly, whooping like madmen.

Prentiss dived out of the wheelhouse as a burst of fire erupted above his head. He fired his silenced pistol and one of the boarders was blasted off his feet. From the other end of the ship, Breckenridge and Hill raced along firing their Ingrams from the hip as they came. The boarders fired back, but fired high. They went down in a heap. At almost the same moment, Hill and Breckenridge heard the 'dead man's click' from their weapons. Their magazines were empty.

'Out of fucking ammo!' Breckenridge yelled. 'That was the last we had!'

The PT boats were moving in again, a storm of gunfire preceding them.

'Cut that bloody scramble net free!' Willan yelled. 'Take the weapons from those bodies. See how much ammo they've got on them.'

Geary raced up and began sawing at the

tough fibres of the scramble net with his knife while Breckenridge and Hill searched the broken bodies of the dead boarders for weapons and ammunition. Willan joined them. The pain was becoming worse now, making him gasp for breath. But he saw something among the bodies that made him reach through the blood and shattered flesh to pull it out.

Prentiss had returned to the helm and was fighting to bring the ship back under control. He whistled down the ancient speaking tube that ran to the engine-room and demanded more steam from the stokers. The old steamer was already flat out, but she was losing speed because of the hundreds of bullet holes in her stack, which meant that it was less efficient at providing an up-draught.

The port PT boat closed in again. There was another crash as she struck the *Victoria*'s hull, and a dozen men leapt from her decks on to the scramble net and began hauling themselves up.

Bullets by the hundred smashed into the side of the steamer. The SBS men had no choice but to cower behind the steel bulkhead of the ship's rail. Geary was still sawing at the scramble net as the faces of the first boarders came up over the ship's side.

A burst of AK47 fire threw them off again. Hill had taken one of the earlier boarders' weapons and fired it now at every head which popped up over the ship's side. The scramble net, with its load of attackers, slipped, frayed and finally came apart as Geary sawed away at it with his knife like a maniac. It fell free of the ship with its cargo of screaming men, and plunged into the lake.

'Must get this fucker sharpened,' Geary said, white-faced. Hill grinned at him.

The attacking boats were closing in again on both sides now, fire from their crews raking the steamer from stem to stern. The one to port soon sheered off, however, turning back to pick up the crowd of men who had fallen into the lake along with the scramble net.

The starboard attacker was the one with the Browning. The heavy gun punched holes clean through the steel sides of the steamer. Prentiss found himself flat on the deck again as the wheelhouse was blasted to wreckage around him. The *Victoria* began to slow down as the damage took its toll; some of the heavy-calibre rounds had gone through the hull and punctured her boilers.

Willan propped himself up, an AK47 in his bandaged hands. He was breathing heavily but his head was clear. He called out to the other SBS men.

'See if you can't give me a little covering fire to distract those bastards, lads. I've got a surprise for them.'

'Anything you say, Sarge. But this is our last throw,' Geary answered.

Geary and the others leapt up and began laying down a curtain of automatic fire on the starboard PT boat. They had gleaned weapons and a couple of magazines apiece from the enemy dead, but they would last only a few seconds.

Willan stood up and took careful aim, ignoring the pain in his hands. He had only one shot, and he must not miss.

Attached to the end of his AK47 was a rifle grenade. He aimed it at the wooden hull of the enemy PT boat, adjusted for the slight roll of the ship, then fired.

His shoulder was shoved backwards by the heavy recoil. He staggered.

The grenade went in on target, punching through the wooden hull of the enemy vessel as though it were cardboard. There was a muffled explosion, then a louder one, and a chunk of the PT boat's hull detonated outwards.

The vessel swerved round as the water

began to fill her hull. It happened frighteningly quickly. She toppled over, men screaming and jumping clear of her deck. Seconds later she capsized entirely, and gurgled rapidly from sight, leaving only a bubbling disturbance to mark her passing, and the bobbing heads of a score of men who were treading water and clinging to fragments of wreckage.

The Ugandans had had enough. The other boat, having picked up some of its own crew from the water, now stopped to pick up survivors from its sister ship. The pursuit was abandoned. A few volleys of shots were fired by way of a last defiance, but the *Victoria* limped away unmolested.

Willan collapsed to the deck. The pain was eating through the comfortable numbness that the morphine had engendered.

Geary bent over him.

'Sarge? Sarge? That was a fucking marvellous shot, by the stupidest cunt I've ever had the privilege to meet.'

'Pleasure's all mine,' Willan groaned.

'We'll get you to a hospital soon. Bukoba's only a few hours away. We made it, Sarge. We did it.'

'Some of us did,' Willan said.

The world closed in on him and became dark. The bright sky and the chugging engines of the steamer disappeared. Even the pain died away.

15

Admiral Leighton sipped his coffee in silence. The ubiquitous Whitehall traffic thundered past outside, never ceasing. It was raining, a cold, dull day in December, the afternoon already turning winter-dark.

Warm enough in here, though, with the fire burning brightly in the grate. How many civil servants had an open fire in their office? he wondered.

The door to the room opened and a grey-haired man in a suit entered. Leighton stood up as he entered but the other man waved him back down again, placed a slim briefcase by the desk and helped himself to coffee from the silver pot. Then he took his seat, facing Leighton, and began flipping through the file which the admiral had placed there a few minutes ago.

'Sorry to keep you waiting, Leighton. So this is the update on the Tanzanian situation, eh?'

'Yes. You'll find it's quite thorough. Your man Prentiss has cooperated completely with Naval Intelligence. I have to thank you for loaning him to us.'

'Not at all, not at all.' The civilian flipped shut the file after a cursory glance at its contents and leant back in his richly upholstered chair, sipping at his coffee.

'Why don't you give me a verbal summary before I delve into the thick of it? How have things gone? Your own opinion, of course.'

Leighton bowed his head a moment, mustering his thoughts.

'We brought our people – those who had survived – out of the country a month ago,' he said slowly. 'Four of them died . . .'

'I'm sorry to hear that.'

'Four of them died and one was so badly wounded – burns, mostly – that he will probably be invalided out of the service.'

'I say, rotten luck. Rather high casualties, though. What exactly was their role in the whole affair? You have to remember that the briefings I get are not as detailed as all that, Leighton. I have to keep a grip of the bigger picture.'

A muscle flickered in the admiral's jaw.

'Of course. Well, largely speaking, their

mission was a success. They trained up a substantial force of Ugandan exiles and Tanzanians and used them to blunt the main thrust of Amin's invasion – taking high casualties as they did so. Prior to this they had also crippled the lakeside raiders, who had been a thorn in Tanzania's side for quite some time. In this previous operation they had captured some kind of antiquated steamer which, subsequent to the invasion, they took to Entebbe – on our orders. Operating out of this, they destroyed three-quarters of Amin's air force on the ground, thus ending the bombing of Tanzanian towns . . .'

'Good show,' the man on the other side of the desk said approvingly.

'Two of them died in this operation. The rest made it back to Tanzania, where we had them airlifted out within days, discreetly. Unfortunately, with the heat and the unhygienic conditions, the team leader's condition deteriorated to the extent that he could not be fully rehabilitated.'

'Damned shame.'

'Quite. I was thinking of some kind of gong for the surviving men. Just something to mark what they have achieved.'

The other man shook his head. 'Afraid

not, Leighton. That sort of thing would beg questions. What was the medal for? What have they done to get it? No, I'm sorry, but they'll have to make do with the gratitude of their country. After all, they were doing what they were paid to do.'

The muscle twitched again in Leighton's jawline. 'Quite,' he said with icy politeness.

'Good. I'm glad we see eye to eye on that one. Now, tell me about the current situation with regard to Tanzania and Uganda. I'm a little behind, you understand. Everything seems geared towards Northern Ireland these days.'

'The Tanzanian Army has been on the offensive for nearly three weeks now,' Leighton said coldly. 'It has pushed the Ugandans away from the Kagera and they are in retreat back to their own borders.'

'Excellent.'

'Yes. Nyerere has sworn to see Amin topple. It is now generally recognized that the Tanzanians will not stop once they have reclaimed their territory. They are going to keep going until they take Kampala.'

The civilian blinked. 'Is it possible, do you think?'

Leighton shrugged. 'No one thought it

possible that Amin's army could be brought to a halt in the first place, let alone thrown into retreat. The defence of the Kagera salient by the SBS-trained battalion was a great boost to the morale of the country. The militias have mushroomed, and they have the men to train them now, thanks to that team of ours.'

'Indeed. They did sterling service.'

'Speaking of the men, I have a request to make,' the admiral said.

'By all means.'

'I wish to retrieve the bodies of the four men who died in Africa, of one of them in particular. He was married, and his wife is naturally keen to bury her husband's body.'

'What have you told relatives and dependants of the deaths?'

'A training accident. A helicopter went down at sea.'

'Well, then they can hardly expect to get the bodies, can they?'

'Sir, this is a matter of . . . of honour. Those men served their country to the best of their ability, and made the ultimate sacrifice. The least we can do is give them a decent burial.'

'No. I'm afraid it's quite out of the question, Admiral. From what you say, two of the men were lost in Uganda. We can hardly go cap in hand to Amin asking for the bodies of our servicemen when they weren't supposed to be there in the first place. And that's another thing . . .'

Here the grey-haired man reached into his briefcase, took out a newspaper and passed it across the desk to Leighton.

'What's this – the *Sydney Herald*?'

'Look at the headline.'

'"British Special Forces Fight In Africa – How the British Are Bringing Down Amin." Who wrote this?'

'An Australian journalist named Susan Morris. Apparently she was in Tanzania at the same time as your team.'

Leighton read the leader article. 'It's accurate, if sensationalist.'

'Yes. We're putting pressure on the Aussies to shut her up. It shouldn't prove a problem, but I want you to be aware, Leighton, of the difficulties involved in keeping our role in this . . . discreet.'

Leighton tossed the newspaper back on the desk. He looked suddenly weary.

'Very well then. We'll keep to the official line. A helicopter accident, the bodies unrecoverable.'

'There's a good chap. It's in the best interests of the country, after all. Now, I wanted to have a word with you about sending some of your specialists to Northern Ireland. There's been a lot of gun-running going on across the lakes in Fermanagh . . .'

The Tanzania file was pushed to one side and the two men leant forward to debate the deployment of more of their subordinates. While the December drizzle poured down outside they concocted plans which would ultimately send the men of the SBS into harm's way again. It was, after all, what they were paid to do.

16

On 11 April 1979 the capital of Uganda, Kampala, fell to troops of the Tanzanian Defence Force and the Ugandan National Liberation Front. Idi Amin escaped and became an exile in Saudi Arabia. When the Tanzanians withdrew, as they had said they would when they had rid the country of Amin, a new civil administration was set up. Tito Okello was promoted to brigadier general and commander-in-chief of the Ugandan Army. Yusufu Lule, an exiled intellectual, was elected president of the new Uganda. Between them they had the task of rebuilding a shattered country and a destroyed economy, and of looking after over a million orphans whose parents had been murdered by Amin's regime.

The bodies of Privates Michael Morgan,

Anthony Parker, James Fraser and John Gordon of the SBS were never recovered. Officially, their deaths were put down to a training accident.

Sergeant John Willan eventually recovered from his wounds and left the service, discharged disabled. In the sergeants' mess at Poole, it is rumoured that he returned to Africa as a mercenary, and was killed in Angola a year later. His body was never found.

OTHER TITLES IN SERIES FROM 22 BOOKS

Available now at newsagents and booksellers
or use the order form provided

continued overleaf . . .

All at £4.99

22

All 22 Books are available at your bookshop, or can be ordered from:

'22' BOOKS Cash Sales Department
P.O. Box 11, Falmouth
Cornwall TR10 9EN
Tel: +44(0) 1328 374900
Fax: +44(0) 1328 374888
E-mail: book@barni.avel.co.uk

POST AND PACKING:
Payments can be made as follows: cheque, postal order (payable to 22) or by credit cards. Do not send cash or currency.

UK orders (1 book only)	£1.50
UK orders (2 books or more)	**FREE OF CHARGE**
E.E.C. & Overseas	25% of order value

NAME (Block Letters) _____

ADDRESS _____

_____

Post/zip code_____

☐ Please keep me in touch with future **22** publications

☐ I enclose my remittance for _____

☐ I wish to pay by Visa/Access/Mastercard/Eurocard

Card Expiry Date

_____